THE
LAST
LIE

A REDD HERRING NOVEL

THE
LAST
LIE

DAVID GEIMAN

WHALER
BOOKS

Buena Vista, VA

1 3 5 7 9 10 8 6 4 2

Library of Congress Control Number: 2025907959

The Last Lie
David Geiman

p. cm.
1. Fiction: Mystery & Detective—General
2. Fiction: Mystery & Detective—Police Procedural
3. Fiction: Thrillers—Crime

I. Geiman, David, 1944– II. Title.
ISBN 13: 978-1-966392-05-7 (hardcover : alk. paper)
ISBN 13: 978-1-966392-04-0 (softcover : alk. paper)
ISBN 13: 978-1-966392-06-4 (ebook)

Design and Layout by Karen Bowen

Whaler Books
An imprint of
Mariner Media, Inc.
131 West 21st Street
Buena Vista, VA 24416
Tel: 540-264-0021
www.marinermedia.com

Printed in the United States of America

This book is printed on acid-free paper meeting the requirements of the American Standard for Permanence of Paper for Printed Library Materials.

Dedicated to all who still read books.

Contents

Prologue 1

Marta Miller opened her laptop once more, knowing that there would be no message for her from either her husband or her son. Nathan had left the week before Christmas, headed to London as his first stop.

Nathan had always been a wild card—dabbled with drugs, drank too much, could not hold a job. She blamed herself but blamed Tom more. The apple had not fallen far from that tree.

When they hadn't heard from Nathan for several days, she could tell Tom was becoming more anxious, but both father and son had done dicey things before, and she was not deeply concerned. It was Tom's idea to go and look for him. It was the holidays, and she had gifts to wrap and meals to prep. Tom had left alone without delay. Now Marta had the house to herself.

When Tom reported that he had not seen Nathan in London and was going on to Amsterdam where Nathan had mentioned connections, she was not surprised. When Tom stopped replying to texts, she decided she needed to do something. She called a man she knew well, their representative in Congress, Bob Graves, a Republican and long-time conservative. He owed her on several levels, not the least of which was the occasional tryst at the Boar's Head Inn in Charlottesville. They were both bored with their spouses but so far still with them. She would joke with Bob that the sex was quite good for a Republican, and he took the ribbing in good humor. He was much more adventurous in bed than her husband, and they both got off on the thrill of cheating.

When she finally got through to Bob, he at first asked her why she didn't just let Tom go missing, as little as she liked him. He quickly adjusted his approach when she didn't take the joke well. He was in Florida for the Christmas break, and from the background noises, she imagined him to be with another conquest, but she let it go. He promised to call someone at the State Department or the FBI, and that satisfied her.

Prologue 2

Gabe Dunbar could not believe his luck. He had wanted to get Sandy into bed for as long as he had known her. The sheer good luck of her divorce—bad luck for her, of course, and for the husband—and the timing, with his wife out of town and Sandy needing to do family research in Albemarle County. He didn't realize she came from Albemarle stock.

The exchange of emails, out of the blue, the date set, at a convenient time—almost as if she had the liaison in mind from the beginning. The very thought of that was enough to boost his already substantial ego. And he had to admit, for a man approaching thirty, he thought he looked pretty good. Not a touch of grey like a classmate he knew, no thinning of the hair, jaw and chin muscles still tight, and stomach flat from thrice-weekly workouts at the gym and weekend golf and tennis.

They had dinner at a place in Charlottesville where he sometimes dined with his legal clients and where his presence with an attractive woman would not arouse suspicion. His wife knew Sandy from college days, so she could be introduced as a mutual friend.

He put her carry-on bag and backpack in the cozy guest room of the large white Georgian house just off highway 250 leading into town from the west. She had arranged her own taxi from the airport and said she would rent a car in the next day or so to do some family research.

After dinner, they made polite conversation in the sitting room off the kitchen while they sipped on an Oregon Pinot Noir. He made inquiries as to the nature of her research. She responded in amusing terms—warm-up for verbal foreplay—the glances, the signaling of some desire.

When she was ready to head up to her room, Gabe escorted her, and they kissed by the bed. They stripped down to underwear quickly. She hesitated for a moment and went into the bathroom, closing the door. He took off his boxers and slid into bed, not registering the hesitation as anything more than a normal bathroom break. She was back in a few minutes with a towel to place beneath them while they had sex. Just to be safe, she had said.

The sex was good, but not as good as he had hoped. Probably nervousness on her part. She did know his wife. After he finished, too quickly, she indicated that she preferred to sleep alone but that they could give it another whirl in the morning. He left her reluctantly and heard her lock the guestroom door as he walked down the hall to his and his wife's bedroom. Not as thrilling as he had hoped, but still, he had finally screwed Sandy, hot, hot Sandy. An old memory flashed in his head.

1

Missing Persons

It was the first of the year, and Reddford Herring was spending his early mornings driving a John Deere tractor with a heated cab and a comfortable seat. He was picking up hay bales from a large covered barn and putting them in feeders for a group of prize Angus heifers on his now heavily-committed girlfriend, Kathryn Ashby's, working farm west of Staunton, Virginia. The previous year had been unusually dry, and pastures were thin. They had been feeding hay longer than normal, and the cost of hay had gone up dramatically. For now, they had an ample supply from the past years of cuttings.

Until recently, Redd had been the sheriff of Augusta County and, even more recently, a special investigation resource for the FBI, or at least for Wendell Berry, his long-time FBI contact and friend. Moving the hay was pleasant and satisfying work, especially compared to the unpleasantness and ingrained evil he had discovered in the two crime cases he had closed out before Christmas.

There were definitely still some loose ends, but a certain justice seemed to have prevailed. The constant themes were greed and plain old human weakness, sometimes driven by the practices of the day and society's view of what constituted crime or sin. Sex, money, and love, most always.

Redd had grown up on a farm, and while the military and law enforcement had been his careers, he still had a place in his heart for farming and cattle. In many ways, Katherine's farm was simple to operate, except during sale days in the autumn, when the cattle had to be prepped and shown to buyers. The rest of the year they were moved from pasture to pasture, as they ate down the growth of mixed grasses.

In calving season, the cows were checked twice daily and new calves given shots and identification tags and tattoos. The breeding heifers and cows were generally artificially inseminated on a seasonal basis. Kathryn had worked closely with the animals for years now, and she handled them gently and with little stress. She was also a genetics professor at the University of Virginia, where she was currently developing a new research project, and she had grown very pleased with Redd's assistance on the farm.

By midmorning, he had finished setting out the hay and checked on a group of cows in the pasture furthest from the main barns. There were bears coming down from the mountains, probably in search of food, and while the cows seemed not to be bothered by them, the bears could easily kill a calf. These cows were not yet due to calve but would be moved as they got closer to a calving date.

Redd had left his phone at Kathryn's house, as usual now. He had decided that having it with him all the time was a distraction, and he wanted to concentrate more on what he was doing as he was doing it. It was a bit new-age, or counter-trendy, or whatever you wished to call it, but unless he needed to be in touch with Kathryn or an investigation was under way, he didn't need to be alerted to events worldwide, or even local, on a constant basis. He hadn't grown up with this kind of information overload and was surviving well without it again.

When he got to the house, he parked his old pickup and went in through the side patio to the kitchen and found a message on his phone to call Wendell Berry. He clicked the return-call icon, and Berry answered immediately.

"What's with you and the phone these days?" Berry asked.

"Good morning to you, too. I leave it at the house when I'm out doing real work," Redd replied.

"Ha! This new country gentleman life is making you soft."

"Give me a break. What's your problem this morning?" Redd asked.

"Missing person."

"Oh crap."

"Well, missing persons, really. Father and son," said Berry.

"Missing where?"

"Did you really ask that?"

"You know what I mean. Where are they missing from, or to?"

Berry sighed. "They're actually missing *from* your area, down by Lexington, I think, and missing *in* Europe, we think—or at least that's what the wife thinks anyway."

"Any specific place in Europe? I ask at the risk of a snide response."

"We know the beginning of their supposed itinerary and not much else. They disappeared. One after the other."

"Say that again. What's the one after the other?"

"It's two disappearances," said Berry. "The son went missing, or at least didn't respond to calls or texts or emails and didn't return when he was supposed to. Then dad went looking for him, and now he is missing."

"Why hasn't this been turned over to the embassies or to the European agencies?"

"It was, and nothing came of it. Of course, I don't think much effort went into it either. There isn't any evidence of foul play—it's not like sex trafficking or anything like that—just a couple of Americans who aren't reporting back to mom."

"So how did this come to your attention?" Redd asked.

"How do you think? The usual. The disappeared person was a party donor, and a congressman's office called us and asked for help. It's outside my remit, but I thought I'd turn it over to you. It is a bit mystifying. And I did a little background checking, and there are some things that don't add up. I suspect one or the other got into something over their heads."

"How about a hint?"

"On the surface, maybe art smuggling. I'm not sure. I don't know enough about it to really comment. But maybe something more. I don't think people get kidnapped or eliminated over artwork, but who knows."

"Once upon a time, you could be burned at the stake for it," Redd replied. "Or so I have read."

"We aren't back there yet," said Berry. "I'm emailing you a file and the contact info for the wife. Let me know whatever else you need."

Berry clicked off, and Redd went into the home office and library to turn on his computer.

2

Musee D'Orsay

Just up the road from the Gabriel Dunbar residence, Kathryn was in her office at the university typing out the final details of the new study she wanted her senior seminar to work on. The project was one involving the damage to telomeres, one of her key areas of concentration. There was more and more evidence of the damage done to chromosomes from long-term stress, from racial and cultural demonization, and more subtle types of harassment. It was not just violence and accident that caused pain.

She was behind, which was unusual for her. She and Redd had gone to Paris for Christmas and New Year's. There was not much happening on the farm other than winter feeding and chores, and her cowboys were happy to work extra hours with bonus pay.

The weather in Paris had been unseasonably mild, and they had walked for miles each day. They had gone twice to the Musee D'Orsay, which was just as crowded as ever in spite of the holidays. Redd had become quite interested in the impressionist painters since meeting Kathryn's brother Douglas, a former computer systems designer and a reclusive genius who made stunning quilts out of thousands of pieces of cloth. His quilts were designed to look like some of those impressionist paintings. Just before they left for Paris, Douglas had told them he was working on a new approach, and he would show it to them when they got back. Douglas was out there on the spectrum somewhere, but Kathryn loved him dearly, and he was protective of her. He and Redd had begun to understand and greatly appreciate each other.

Kathryn felt that her life right now was possibly as good and certainly as happy as it had ever been. She was in love with Redd, appreciated his quiet strength, his lack of pretension, and his willingness to learn. He was not threatened by her wealth. Though not as worldly as Kathryn, Redd was intelligent and had previously appreciated a bit of exposure to some art and cultural institutions such as Musee D'Orsay, thanks to his late wife, Mary's, teaching career. He was enjoying a deeper experience in the art world with Kathryn. She wondered occasionally what Mary Herring had been like. She had died of cancer. Kathryn thought she would have liked Mary, partly because she had been smart enough to choose a man like Redd.

3

Gabe

Gabe had fallen asleep quickly after the drinking and the sex. He had dreamed about sex, but not with Sandy, with some woman he couldn't place who resembled Sandy but who kept fading in and out of the dream. At one point in the night he thought her heard a door closing and footsteps, but decided it was something in the dream and fell back asleep.

Gabe got up at seven the next morning. He thought about walking down the hall to Sandy's room but decided against it. He went to his own bathroom and took a shower and then dressed for the office. He was an attorney, and he still believed in dressing in suit and tie, even on days when no clients were due to come in for an appointment. He didn't have a court appearance that day but would be working on questions for an upcoming deposition, and had a meeting with a client in Culpeper, a small town up Route 29 toward Washington.

He still did not hear any noise coming from upstairs, no toilet flushing or water running. Maybe Sandy slept late. He would need to let her know he was leaving soon. He popped a slice of whole wheat bread into the toaster and poured himself a small glass of orange juice and a cup of coffee from the machine that he had set up *the night before. When the toast popped up he spread it with butter and honey and ate it while sitting at the counter and looking on his iPhone at the sports scores and headlines from the night before.*

When he was finished with the breakfast, he put the dishes in the dishwasher, washed his hands at the prep sink and dried them with a kitchen towel. Still no noise from upstairs.

He went first to his home office which was just around the corner from the kitchen and which had a window that looked out on the northeast side of the house to flower beds and shrubs at the property edge. It was a lovely morning room, especially in summer when the sun was further north in the sky. He put several files into his Tumi attaché case, closed it, and spun the locks. He set it down by the door in the front hallway and went upstairs to awaken Sandy and to give her a key to the house. She would obviously be leaving later than he had expected, and he didn't know when she would return. His wife, Celia, was not due back for three more days.

Her bedroom door was still shut, and there were no sounds coming from the room or the bathroom. He tapped lightly on the door and got no response. He knocked louder and still got no response, so he tried the knob and found that it turned. He was sure he had heard her lock it the night before when he left.

The room was still in shadow due to the room-darkening curtains that Celia had installed to block the early morning sun so that guests could sleep longer if they wished. He slid the light dimming switch up so as not to startle Sandy and was surprised to find the bed empty. The bathroom door was ajar, but the light was off in there. He called her name, but there was no response. He went to the bathroom, pushed the door completely open, and turned on the lights. She was not there.

He turned and looked around the bedroom. Her suitcase was still on the folding stand that Celia had bought for the guest room. Her backpack was on a chair. He looked back into the bathroom and saw her toiletries out and on the counter.

It made no sense. Clothes were spilling out of the suitcase, as if she had been looking for a particular thing to wear, and the backpack also seemed to have been dumped. There were shoes on the floor and a pair of panties and a bra, the ones she had been wearing the night before, were on the floor beside the bed. He walked to the bed and pulled back the top sheet and blanket. There was no sign of the large towel she had insisted they put on the bed the prior evening. Maybe she had put it in the laundry basket or washing machine.

He looked in the closet. She had hung up a nice dress, short skirt, and a blouse, all looking quite new. There was also the coat she had worn the night before. But no Sandy. Maybe she was a sleep-walker and had gone into another bedroom? It seemed farfetched, but he walked along the hallway and opened the doors to the two other bedrooms on that floor and looked in. No sign of her. He went to the third floor where there was a large finished room that was used as storage, but as expected she wasn't there. He needed to leave for the office.

She surely must have gotten up early and gone for an early morning run? She hadn't mentioned it last night, but then again, other things were on both their minds.

He finally remembered that he had her cell phone number and texted her. There was no response. He tried to call the number, and it went straight to voicemail with a message that no message account had been set up. He really did need to leave now. He was taking someone with him to Culpeper, and they needed to get some work done prior to leaving.

He had forgotten to set the house alarm the night before, but decided he would set it now and lock up. He tested the codes he had given Sandy for the garage and the inside door, so she could get in when she got back from her run or wherever she had gone. His wife had valuable jewelry and some of their artwork had value. He was not about to leave the house unlocked.

He was becoming quite irritated by now and wondered what Sandy was up to. She had always been a bit wild and unpredictable, but this was crazy and exceptionally inconsiderate. He flashed back to the sex the night before and was nudged to a higher level of irritation when he thought how unremarkable and, truthfully, unsatisfying and almost perfunctory it had been. He had been slightly drunk, and in the clearer air of morning realized he had been used the night before for a quick screw. That would usually be the male's idea of a fun evening, but she had turned the tables on him, and it pissed him off.

He texted her, locked up, and left for the office.

4

Another Woman

At the Holiday Inn Express a short mile from Gabe's house, a woman in sweatpants with reddish hair had checked in the afternoon before and had asked about the times for the airport shuttle the following morning. The woman had a cough and was wearing a mask. The front desk told her there was a shuttle at 4:30 a.m. which would take passengers for the 6:00 a.m. flights to Chicago and Atlanta. She booked a space on it.

The clerk did not see her again in person that evening, but there were entrances to the parking lot that could be accessed with the room keys. He may have spotted her going out and coming in on the security camera on several occasions but there was really nothing to draw attention to her other than the cough, and she checked out at 4:25 that morning and caught the shuttle to the airport. She was still coughing and wearing the mask.

5

So Concerned

Berry's assistant sent along the basic contact information for Marta Miller and a short attached file with information on her missing husband and son. There was a post-it saying more information would follow in a day or two. To Redd's surprise, Marta appeared to not have taken her husband's name, but the son had. Her husband's name was Thomas McFerren, and the son's name was Nathan McFerren. The McFerren name rang a tiny bell—some fraud and a bankruptcy. There was nothing in the file to explain the difference in names, but he supposed it could be a second marriage or a modern marriage with no name change desired.

He decided to give Mrs. Miller a call and get some background. She answered on the second ring.

"Mrs. Miller, this is Reddford Herring, a special investigator for the FBI calling. Is this Mrs. Marta Miller?"

"Yes, yes—has something happened? Have you found them?"

"No, no, I don't have any information. I was just asked a short time ago to look into this matter."

"Oh, I see. And who are you?"

Redd explained his role and how he had been given the assignment.

"I see. So what do you need from me? I am quite worried, especially about my son. I just know something has happened when they both disappeared like this."

"I understand. Have they ever disappeared before?"

"Oh no, nothing like this. Never both of them. Nathan goes off a little every now and then. But never both. I just don't understand what could have happened."

Redd sensed that he wasn't going to get anywhere with a phone call. Mrs. Miller was fixated, understandably, on what might be the worst-case scenario. Getting trip and behavior details would best be done in person. "Mrs. Miller, the information I have shows your address as Long Hill Road, south of Lexington. Is that correct?"

"Yes."

"I have GPS directions that show an entrance off of Old Mine Road and a long lane, it seems?"

"Yes, that is it."

"So, how about I head down to see you in about forty-five minutes? I need to do a bit of prep."

"Yes, please, that would be very kind of you. I am so anxious and so concerned."

"I understand. I will be there in, let's see, probably two hours from now."

She thanked him, and he clicked off.

He had typed the name Thomas McFerren into the computer while talking to Mrs. Miller, and now he could see why the name had rung the tiny bell. McFerren had been involved in a major insurance scandal involving industrial properties in Richmond. He narrowly escaped going to prison for fraud. There had also been several bankruptcies in Augusta County and surrounding counties involving rental properties, and some complicated financing arrangements. McFerren definitely had a worrisome past.

There was not much on the younger McFerren, just a listing for Native American art appraisals and a link to a gallery site, but that site would not come up when Redd clicked the link. When Redd checked another database he still had access to from a former case, there didn't appear to be any criminal record for Nathan.

Redd decided not to print off the material he had found, but to wait and see what Mrs. Miller brought up in a conversation. That might shed more light on what her husband and son were involved in now. He didn't want to suggest anything.

He took a shower and dressed in grey slacks, a blue-checked pinpoint Oxford shirt, and a light blue blazer, a combination that was professional in appearance but not harsh or threatening. Kathryn had suggested that he might want to dress a little more elegantly, partly because it pleased her. It wasn't that he'd been dowdy in the first place, or at least that was what he chose to believe. He was becoming comfortable with the clothes, but he was not going to give up his truck.

6

Marta Miller

It took Redd a little over an hour to drive south on the interstate to an exit just beyond Lexington and meander around small roads as directed by the app on his phone. He found the driveway, which was flanked by two brick pillars with planters on top. The plants were in need of trimming. The unattended, dead summer flowers of some spiky variety now drooped over the edges, dark and moldy-looking.

The driveway was paved and curved gently to the right and was set in the middle of a grassy avenue leading to a huge three-story house that looked like a junior version of some English country estate. There were six chimneys, four square white columns holding up a Jeffersonian-looking overhang to the front of a roof that sported three wide dormers on each side. The house was so out of place, he couldn't understand it. It belonged in the hunt country northeast of Charlottesville or by Upperville and the fancy horse country outside of Washington. It didn't fit in down here in the country where the nearest houses were one-story ranchers with three small bedrooms, an above ground pool, and two mortgages. There was no one to lord it over around here.

He pulled up close to the front door of the house on a circular driveway with a fountain in the middle, now covered for winter with a tarp tied to the base. Redd got out and looked around at the view. Not bad, with the Allegheny mountains in the distance to the west and the Blue Ridge foothills being around the other side. It was a great place for a house, just less of one.

He walked to the front door and pushed a brass button to ring the bell. He half expected a tuxedo-clad butler to open the door, but in a moment, an attractive, dark-haired woman who he guessed to be a well-preserved fifty or so opened the door. She was dressed in an expensive-looking pantsuit that fit snugly and showed off a nice figure, high firm breasts, maybe a touch too firm, and a firm derriere. She either had had work done or had never had wrinkles by her eyes, which were a deep grey. She was still cute, a round pixie-ish look to her face, which might not age well, but that would probably depend on the quality of future enhancements.

She extended her hand and said, "Good afternoon. Mr. Herring, I hope."

"Yes, Mrs. Miller. Redd Herring."

"Please call me Marta—I don't feel like Mrs. Miller. In fact, I changed my name back to my maiden name, so I suppose you could call me Miss Miller, now that I think about it. Dull though, isn't it? 'Miller'? I should have been born with a better name. Oh well, too late."

They were still standing by the door, and a cold breeze was chilling the hall. Redd was attempting not to look at the effect the cold had on Mrs. Miller's breasts, easily seen through the silk blouse she wore with the pants suit. Obviously she wore no bra. Redd thought back to his last case and wondered where all of these sexy women were coming from.

"I'm here to talk about your husband and son, Marta, so is

there somewhere we could possibly sit and you could give me a bit of background?"

"Oh, of course, come this way. It's a bit chilly here, and I have a fire in the morning room. I know it's not morning anymore, but it's close to the kitchen." Redd had no idea why that mattered.

"This is a remarkable house, especially for around here."

"Oh, it certainly is, isn't it? Would you like a tour? My husband got it for a song."

"Not right now, thank you. Maybe another time. I'm surprised though, to see something so grand around here. There must not be another like it in the valley."

"That could be. The old guy who had it built was really weird, I guess. He made a bunch of money on a patent for some special lawn mower or something and then went off his rocker a little bit and thought he was descended from some baron or duke or lord or whatever from England and built the house to prove it. I don't know why he didn't just move to England and buy one."

"Strange," said Redd. They had entered a tastefully decorated room down the central hallway to the right. Like the rest of the first floor, the ceiling was high, perhaps twelve feet, and a fire was burning in a large brick-lined fireplace on the west wall, while to the east, large windows looked out to the mountains and a terrace which could be accessed through French doors. The room had two large couches, several comfortable-looking wing chairs, and a collection of lamps on tables. A designer had clearly been at work.

"Please have a seat by the fire. Would you like something to drink, a glass of wine, a beer?"

"No, no, nothing for me. But go ahead."

"No, I'll wait for now. Thank you for coming to see me so quickly."

"Why don't you go ahead and tell me what the situation is with your husband and son. It is your husband and son, I take it. You mentioned a name change?"

"Oh yes. Well, that was after that business with the trumped-up charges against Tom over the insurance. I suppose you know about that."

"Not much. Why don't you fill me in?" Marta Miller seemed to be all over the place thought-wise, and so far there wasn't much evidence of concern about her husband and son. "Or rather, why don't you tell me about your husband and son, and then we can cover other things if needed."

"Of course, of course. You know, I think I will just have a small glass of Chardonnay, to steady my nerves." She laughed nervously as she stood back up and went to a drinks trolley by a door that must have led to the kitchen or a breakfast room. Who knew how many functions rooms might be assigned in this strangely misplaced house. Redd wondered if Sandy had been a model at some point, noting the way she stood as she poured the wine from a bottle already chilled in a silver bucket. She had one foot turned out, the better to display her profile, and her low heels had done what heels are supposed to do—push out and round an already lovely ass.

Redd looked away to the crackling fire and smiled to himself. Kathryn, a confident natural beauty in her own right, would find all of this amusing.

"Now, sorry, you must be very busy, and I am just holding you up. I do appreciate you coming so quickly. I don't mean to seem so flaky. It's just that I am really worried about both of them."

"I'm all ears."

"Okay, it started back after Thanksgiving. My son, Nathan, told us he was going to England and maybe several other cities in Europe—I don't recall all the details now—to set up arrangements to sell Native American paintings. I guess those kinds of paintings are very much in demand in Europe these days. No idea why, but he claims it to be the case."

"Just a clarification—your son's last name is McFerren, is that right? Nathan McFerren."

"Yes, and his dad is Tom McFerren."

"And you are still married?"

"Yes, I just did the name change-back after that awful insurance business so that I could get a credit card in my name and not have to deal with all the aftermath, you know."

"I understand. Alright, go ahead, your son left for Europe to sell artworks. Did he take a lot of inventory with him?" Redd asked this question because he hadn't found a working online link to a gallery, which made him wonder about the younger McFerren's depth of knowledge and professionalism.

"No, he wasn't taking paintings and such with him, or I don't think so. I don't really know—I didn't see him before he left. He said he had shipped over some large pieces, already framed and packaged, and he would collect them from a warehouse or some such and visit buyers."

"Had he been in this business long?" asked Redd.

"No, this was something new. Actually, it was really the first *real* business he had become involved in, if you know what I mean."

"No, I really don't know what you mean."

Marta sighed, stood, and went to the drinks cart to refill her glass.

"Why am I bullshitting you? If you know the name McFerren, then you must know about my husband's reputation—his schemes and the fraud trial and the bankruptcies and all of that?"

"I had a quick look this afternoon before heading down here, but I don't know details. It was never part of what I dealt with as a sheriff."

"I see. Well the truth is, I married a con man, and my son has turned out to be one as well, I fear. I was planning to divorce Tom—was getting papers ready—and then Nathan disappeared, and I didn't have the heart for it until he turned up. But he didn't, and then Tom had the bright idea to go look for him. I thought at the time that maybe they had cooked up something between them, but now I don't know. I think they really did go missing or got caught up in something they couldn't control. Tom could charm the pants off the pope, or whatever the pope wears, but neither one of them has ever done much business or scheming in Europe. I just don't know."

"I'm confused. So, is your son really in the art business or isn't he? I looked him up, and there was a link to his gallery, but the link wouldn't work. Does he have a gallery somewhere or not?"

"He was supposedly setting up an online gallery and maybe would do a physical presence sometime in the future. He said it was the trend."

"Alright. It doesn't look as if he got that set up, then. Where was he the last time you heard from him? Was he in Europe?"

"Yes, he had arrived in London and was meeting people there."

"How long was he in London?"

"I'm not sure. Just a couple of days. He told Tom he was going on to Amsterdam on the Chunnel train."

"And he never called you from Amsterdam?"

"No. He told Tom, or I guess he did, that he would be busy for a few days, and we might not hear from him. But how busy can you be to not be able to text a few 'good mornings' or 'good nights,' or a few lines to say you've arrived fine and are staying in so-and-so hotel? You know, the way he did in London."

"You said he didn't have much experience in Europe. Had he traveled or worked there at all before this?"

"I don't know. I don't think he had been there a lot, no work that I know of. His dad had had some investors, if you get my meaning, from Europe, but neither of them know the continent that well. Or England either. I was surprised he was pursuing this. I guess surprised, but pleased that he was maybe for once doing something independent and not with his father, who was not a good influence. I should have divorced him years ago."

Redd wanted to ask her why she hadn't, but that could wait. He needed to organize his thoughts better, and he needed a deep dive on the elder McFerren's background. "Where does your son live?" asked Redd.

"He has an apartment in Charlottesville. I see him some, but Tom sees him more."

Redd thought about asking to see the room he stayed in when he came to visit but decided that would hold little value. "Do you have an itinerary for his planned trip?" he asked.

"No, I know what flight he took from Dulles to London, but nothing else. Oh, and the hotel in London."

"Why did your husband think he could locate Nathan?"

"I don't know—he wouldn't say why. But I think he was flying to London and then on to Amsterdam, or maybe he was flying to Amsterdam direct, then going to London. He seemed to know that Nathan had supposedly taken the train to Amsterdam."

"Can you give me some exact dates? So they were both gone over Christmas, is that right?"

"Yes. Nathan was supposed to be back before Christmas. When he didn't come back and we didn't hear from him, that was a bit more concerning. And the embassies were probably understaffed at Christmas. I tried to get them to do something, but they were useless. Tom left before Christmas. I really don't know what he thought he could accomplish. Unless it's something they're in on together."

"Can you give me his credit card information? We can request some details. Or do you have access to his card or cards—your husband's, I mean?"

"I have access to one but not the others. Can't the FBI just look them up and see what's on them?"

"It depends. It would be most efficient if you could provide something now."

"I think he has cards I don't know about, but we did share a Visa that got miles, and he used that for points a lot. He may have charged some travel on that. I didn't think to look. He always pays the bills."

Herring wondered if that was all true, especially if Mrs. McFerren, Miller, Marta, was going to get a divorce. What was she planning to live on? Did she have separate funds? Too many questions for the moment. He really needed to think this through and come up with a clear approach.

"What do you live on now?" he asked. "What business is your husband in?"

She smiled. "I told you he was a con man. I don't know the details, but each month we get funds into our checking and other accounts from somewhere offshore. He says they are tax-paid, but I have no idea. The IRS hasn't come after him, so I guess it's okay. He hasn't worked for quite a while, but I had a sense we might be running low from whatever the source of our current income is."

Redd had gone looking into offshore accounts in the past when he was sheriff, even before he had the resources of the FBI behind him. But even their resources were not as good as those he alone could now call on from his private source. Douglas, Kathyrn's reclusive brother, had designed many of the sophisticated operating systems in place around the world. He could probably hack into the Defense Department computers if needed and could certainly give Redd a heads-up on how McFerren was moving money around.

"Marta, if you wouldn't mind, can you write down all of the credit card information you do have, along with usernames and passwords and so on? I'll get the FBI to begin looking and see what we can find. I don't suppose you have the same information for your son?"

"No, I'm sorry, I don't. But I can give you his address, and I can meet you there if you want to look around."

"Probably later. Let us get to work on this first." Redd stood up.

"Are you still a sheriff?" asked Marta, getting to her feet. "Weren't you the sheriff in Augusta County? There was that big kidnapping case and a murder case."

"I retired from being sheriff. I do special projects for the FBI now."

"Are you married?" she grinned.

"No, but I am in a relationship, a very good one."

"Oh, too bad. That whole sheriff thing is kind of sexy."

Redd smiled. "If you say so. It's just another title."

Marta grinned back at him. "I doubt that. I'll get that information for you. Do you want to wait or shall I email it? Is that safe?"

"I have a secure email service. You can email it." He handed her a card with the information on it and told her goodbye. A few minutes later he was on the country road back to the interstate. He wondered if anything Marta had said to him was true, or was he being conned by the con man's wife now?

7

That Damn Woman

Gabe was on his way to the office when his cell phone buzzed. He hoped it was Sandy, but instead it was Celia, his wife.

She told him that her uncle had come down with a virus of some sort that morning and she didn't want to be around it, so she was at the airport. She had managed to change her ticket to 1:00 in the afternoon, but was going to standby for one leaving in less than an hour. She should be home by noon if the standby flight panned out.

Gabe panicked and at first couldn't speak, but soon managed to ask a few questions about the uncle and said he would see her later that day. As soon as she clicked off, he called his assistant and told her to cancel the depositions he had set up for that day in Culpeper, that he had something unexpected come up and he would not be in that day.

He pulled over to turn around to head home and texted Sandy again, but still no response.

When he got to the house she wasn't there. He would need to get all evidence of her out of the house in the next few hours. He quickly gathered up all of her clothes and stuffed them into her roller bag and backpack. He stripped the sheets off of the bed and *put them in the washer on a quick wash. He would need to remake the bed and get Sandy's stuff out of the house. If she would just answer her damn phone, he would tell her to check into a hotel and he would bring her belongings to her. Where in the hell was that damn woman?*

He stuffed her toiletries into the backpack as well as he could. He took the backpack and roller bag down and put them in the back of his SUV and pulled down the cover behind the back seat so that they couldn't be seen. He would have to take it to a hotel. He should have put her in one to begin with.

He went back upstairs and realized he had missed the clothes hanging in the closet. He grabbed the coat, dress, skirt, and top and took them downstairs and stuffed them into a grocery bag and took them out to the car and put them in the trunk as well.

He didn't think to look in the hall closet, or to dump the waste-paper baskets. They had a cleaner, so he didn't have a really clear idea of what a cleaning routine might look like. Celia seldom went into the spare bedroom anyway, so as long as it was mostly neat, the cleaning lady would put it right on her next visit.

The sheets were done in thirty minutes, and he pulled them out and put them in the dryer on a fast dry, highest heat. When they were dry, he pulled them out and made the bed, struggling to fit the bottom sheet, but finally pulling it down enough to get it in place. He didn't know that the wide seam on the top sheet went at the head of the bed, so put it on as best he could, smoothed it down, and pulled the covers over it and got them more or less straight. He had forgotten to wash the pillows, and realized the pillowcases might have her smell on them, if Celia were to look that closely. So he stripped them off but then realized he had no idea where the clean ones were. He didn't have time to do them in the washing machine and dry them, so he placed the pillows under the duvet-like cover and pulled it up. He would have to deal with it later. He balled up the pillowcases and stuffed them on the top shelf of the closet. In his rush, he forgot about the towel they had used the night before. He had no idea that Sandy had folded it and left it neatly hanging on the towel heater.

Gabe texted Sandy again and told her not to come to the house, that Celia was on her way home early and he would get her a hotel room. He told her to go to the Sheraton downtown and text him from there. He would bring her clothes to her. It was now nearly noon.

8

Looking Good

It was dark by the time Redd got back to Kathryn's house. Her cowboys had done the evening rounds of chores, and Kathryn would probably walk the pasture with the cows most likely to calve that night. That wasn't really necessary, but she liked seeing the heifers and cows she had developed and worked with from birth. One of the benefits of artificial insemination was that you knew pretty closely when the mother would have her calf. Cattle had a gestation period of between 279 and 292 days, with Angus cattle like Kathyn's at the lower end of the range. Kathryn's seldom went longer than 285 days. And due to low birth weights—a desirable feature for cattle on the range—there were seldom any birthing problems.

They had a dinner of bean soup and a mixed salad with cornbread croutons and sparkling water to drink. Kathryn had a glass of Malbec before dinner, but nothing later. Redd told her about his interview with Marta and about the strange mansion off on a hill in the countryside.

"Well, Redd, I guess I caught you just in time," Kathryn laughed. "You've become a magnet for hot chicks."

"I don't know where they come from," said Redd. "I never used to run into women like her, or maybe I was just obtuse."

"You are quite exotic, you know, being a sheriff and a gunslinger."

Redd laughed. "Yeah, a gunslinger. Everybody in the country is a gunslinger these days. It's not a desirable trait."

"No, you don't get it. I think these women see you as the old-style hero. You're like the John Wayne guy in the movies, understated but strong. A person with character, someone to look up to. Certainly when compared to their husbands, in this case and the last one. Think about it, one was married to a frustrated gay guy, and this one is married to a con man. And you're kind of good looking." Kathryn smiled at him and then started laughing at the perplexed look on his face.

"Well, it is damned distracting."

"Oh, for God's sake, cut it out," said Kathryn as they got up to clear the table. "If you don't enjoy looking good there's something wrong with you."

"That may be, but both her husband and her son seem to have gone missing, unless this is just another con. Which it could be. Some sort of insurance scam again? I don't know. I need to dig into his past scams. I hate this kind of financial stuff."

"Maybe Douglas could help you. We owe him a visit. I want to see what he's up to as well. And I have some books I bought for him about what influenced some of the artists he likes. Fascinating world back then."

"I've already thought about talking to him. Mrs. Miller doesn't really know where their money comes from, she says, so I'd like for Douglas to see what he can find out. I'll ask Wendell first, but this doesn't seem like very high priority to him."

"We could go up to see Douglas tomorrow if you want. I don't have classes until the next day, and it's too early for students to be signing up for individual interviews and evaluations."

"Okay," said Redd. "I'll just check to see what came in from her this evening and do a quick run-through of what I can find on McFerren."

"Fine. Then I better get you in bed and make sure you don't have a reason to roam, Mr. Sheriff," laughed Kathryn.

9

Flight Information

Redd found a short note from Marta in his secure email with the numbers and expiration dates plus security codes for two Visa cards. She had also sent along the usernames and codes for accessing the two cards online for account info as he had requested. Neither one was as complicated as it should have been.

The first account he looked at was solely in her name and had not been used outside the US and covered mostly normal weekly expenses like food and restaurant charges, gasoline, and orders from Amazon. The second account was in both names and showed a charge on United but not the detail.

Marta had forwarded her husband's flight information. From that Redd could put together a basic timeline. She had also sent along the departure date for Nathan and the date of her last communication with him. She had sent screenshots of the texts as well, but that merely reinforced what she had told him.

Dec 18: Nathan departs to London.
Dec 20: Nathan reports he is leaving for Amsterdam.
Last communication from him.

Dec 23: No reports from Nathan for three days now.
Dec 23: Tom, the husband leaves for London.
Dec 25: Tom arrives Amsterdam two days later.
Dec 25–Dec 31: Tom in Amsterdam hotel.
Dec 31: Tom reports by text going to Florence. No charge on card.
Jan 2: Tom texts he is going to Rotterdam. No charge on card, must have used different one or didn't really go. No more texts from either.
Jan 6: Today's date.

In looking at the dates, Redd wondered what the father had hoped to accomplish over the holidays. And why would he have flown to Florence over New Year's Eve and New Year's Day? He doubted many Italian galleries would have been open those days. And certainly not open to an amateur American trying to set up a sales arrangement. None of it made sense.

He would need to do more research into McFerren to see what he could find out about past schemes and his illegal activity. Perhaps that might shed some light on what he and the son were up to now. He also needed access to McFerren's emails and calendar, but his wife didn't have his passwords for those. Sounds like a job for Douglas.

10

Whatever

Celia did make the earlier flight and got a seat in the back row of the plane, but it was a short flight and no delay in the takeoff line from Atlanta, so she landed just before noon. By the time she got her bag—which she had had to gate check—and picked up her car and drove home it was 12:30. Gabe was still there.

"What are you doing home at this hour?" she asked. "Aren't you working today?"

"Uh, yeah," he stammered. "I just had to come home to get some papers I left by mistake."

"You look a little disheveled. Did you party big last night or something? You look a little hungover."

"Maybe a little," he fibbed. "Just something with the guys. Anyway, I gotta go."

"All right, whatever," she said, dismissing him. "I'm not cooking tonight, so let's go out. Call me later."

He let himself into the garage and backed out. He would need to figure out what to do with Sandy and her clothes soon.

11

Blood in the Drain

Gabe decided not to go back to the office since he had told them something had come up. His appetite was gone, but he went by a Starbucks and got a large coffee and headed for the mountains. He hiked in the mountains frequently with Celia. Even in winter, as long as there was no snow or ice on the roads, sections of the parkway were open for cars. He needed to clear his head.

He went south toward the resort at Wintergreen and stopped at an overlook where there was a roadside marker talking about the people who used to live in the hollows down below and about their agricultural practices. He read it without thinking, seeing a stream of meaningless words. How had things gotten to be such a mess in less than twenty-four hours?

He was still looking over the valley when his phone buzzed. It was Celia. "Gabe, where are you? You need to get back here. There's blood in the basement. I called the cops."

"What, what are you talking about?"

"Blood, there is blood in the drain in the basement."

"What were you doing in the basement?"

"What kind of question is that? I heard a drip of some kind, and I finally went down there, and it was coming from the sink *in the utility room and there was this red stain on the floor and it looked like blood. I got scared and called the cops. Get back here. What is going on?"*

"I have no idea. I'm sure it's nothing, some rust stain or something. I'm headed back now."

"Where are you?"

He ignored the question and clicked off. She buzzed him again, but he ignored it. He would need to get the clothes out of the car. What had Sandy done? God, where was she?

He opened the back of the car and took the clothes in the paper bag out of it and opened the roller bag and stuffed them in as well as he could. It was a tight fit with the jacket, but he managed to get it zipped by sitting on it. There was a trail leading down the mountain near the road market, so he took the suitcase and the backpack and carried them down the trail several hundred feet until he came to a clump of wild holly bushes off to the side. He managed to slide both bags in behind the bushes and covered them with some leaves. He would come back and get them when Sandy finally showed up.

He hiked back up to the car, brushed the dirt and leaves off his pants, wiped his shoes as well as he could in the grass at the side of the parking area and headed back to the house. There must have been some old paint stains in the basement and Celia had just panicked. He hoped. It couldn't be blood. But he didn't really want the cops snooping around either. And the timing was making him uneasy. Was Sandy outing him to his wife?

12

Bullshit

By the time Gabe got back to the house there was a police car in the driveway. He pulled in behind it and went in the front door.

Celia was waiting for him by the kitchen with two officers, a man and a woman. "Where have you been? I've been trying over and over to call you!"

"I had the phone on mute while I was driving. I always do that when I drive, you know that."

"Where have you been? You weren't at the office."

"I just drove over to the mountains, clear my head about a case."

"Bullshit," said Celia. "What are you up to? There's blood in the basement."

Gabe started to protest, but the female officer held up her hand and stopped him. "Mr. Dunbar, I'm Lieutenant Franklin, and this is Sergeant Armstrong with me. We need to talk to you and look over the house. We have a technician headed over now, but it looks like there is blood around and in the drain in your basement, and it looks fresh. How did that get there?"

"I have no idea what you're talking about. I haven't been in the basement for days."

Celia was still looking hard at Gabe. "What were you doing in the mountains? You have on your office suit?"

He wanted to tell her to shut up, but that was out. "I told you. I was concerned about a case, and I went to clear my head."

"I called the office. They said you cancelled depositions today."

"I do that all the time." What was she doing? No one needed to know about Sandy's clothes.

Just then the doorbell chimed with one of those Ring Tones, and the Lieutenant sent the Seargent to answer it. It was the technician at the door. He spoke to him quietly for a few moments by the door and then came back to Gabe and Celia.

"I need for the two of you to take a seat here with Sergeant Armstrong," said the Lieutenant. "I will show the technician the basement, and then, if that is blood as we suspect, we need to look over the entire house. Do either of you have anything you want to say before we start?"

Gabe looked at Celia. "No. I have no idea what's going on."

13

Guest Bedroom

Under the gaze of the sergeant, the two of them took seats across from each other at the table. Celia staring daggers at Gabe. She started to speak, but stopped. So far she hadn't stopped to consider what any of her comments might mean, but now she was composing herself.

Gabe asked for a drink of water, and the sergeant allowed him to get it. He started to speak, thought better of it.

A few minutes later the Lieutenant reappeared. "My technician is running a quick test, but is almost certain this is human blood. I'm going to take a look around the house. You stay here with the sergeant."

Franklin glanced into the rooms on the first floor, the living room down the hall, the dining room next-door to Gabe's office, but didn't go in. She pulled on white gloves and then went upstairs. She could be heard opening doors and walking around.

After a few moments, she called down and asked Armstrong to bring the two of them up.

She was standing at the door of the guest bedroom.

"Did someone stay in this room last night?" she asked them.

"No, of course not," said Celia. "Gabe?"

"No," said Gabe. "Uh, no?"

"When was it last cleaned?"

"Last week," said Celia. "Like every week."

"Well there's a stained towel on the towel rack and another one with blood under the sink. I think I need for the two of you to come down to the station with me. Sergeant?"

14

Needlepoint

The next morning, Redd and Kathryn left after checking the cows and giving directions to the cowboys. Redd's work from the day before had helped with stockpiling hay close to pens where it was needed. It was overcast and clouds hung low over the Allegheny ridges. There was mist in the valleys and patches of fog over the streams and eddies. There had been rain a few days before, but not enough to replenish subsoil moisture.

They headed northwest to Monterey, the small town closest to Douglas's mountain home in neighboring Highland County. The tree trunks along the winding road looked black in the low light of the day. Scattered throughout the fields they could see dead pines that had lost their limbs and now stood stark and forlorn.

They drove through town to see if any progress had been made on restoring the famous old hotel there, but it was still closed. Redd made several turns and headed back to the intersection that would take them south to the entrance to Douglas's driveway. It was chained off, but Kathryn had a key. She dropped the chain, and they parked by the concrete-reinforced garage where Douglas kept his pickup truck. The overgrown driveway from there up to the house was blocked from vehicle traffic by large boulders. Douglas had had them placed there after completing the construction of his small energy-efficient house. He was not overly paranoid about intruders. He had little of value to be stolen at the house. But he was also practical and knew that there were meth labs in the hills around him and occasionally unpredictable people wound up and down the county roads.

Kathryn and Redd walked up to the house and were surprised to find Douglas indoors when they arrived. He was usually outside during daylight hours, tending his garden in warm weather or a small greenhouse that he maintained throughout the year. The greenhouse was set into the hillside and bermed to retain warmth without artificial heat. He could not grow flowers in winter, but hardier vegetables were fine growing in there. And he had built a small springhouse that kept his foods cold in warmer months.

Douglas was seated at a table pulling some brightly colored thread through a loosely woven piece of canvas.

"What in the world?" said Kathryn. "Is that needlepoint?"

"So, they did teach you something at that fancy finishing school you attended," he answered without looking up.

"Screw you, brother," responded Kathryn. "Is this a replacement for quilting?"

"For now. I should have thought of this earlier. It provides some of the same challenges, but it may be a bit too simple. I did a little pre-painted canvas to see how I liked it. I guess someone marks an image on a canvas and then faintly paints it and then people stitch over the painting. I decided to just stitch my image without a pattern to guide me, sort of freehand.

"Hello, Redd. You still around?"

"Seems so, how are you?"

"What you see is what you get, as you should know by now. Have you slain any dragons recently?"

"Not since you last helped me. I enjoyed Paris…"

"Oh, that reminds me, I brought you a book about Pissarro and another about the influence of painters on writers in France," interrupted Kathryn. "But I forgot and left them at the house. You'll have to come over and get them."

"That's a cheap trick."

"Honest mistake. May I have some tea?"

"Help yourself. Redd, really, you're saying you don't have any new puzzles for me to solve? You're slipping."

"I didn't really say that. I do have something I need help with. Money coming from offshore and a father and son missing in Europe."

"If they're smart, they'll stay missing in Europe for a while."

"They may be intentionally missing, but it's too early to tell. It might be a con."

"Jeez, you get to work with some great people. But I've said that before."

Kathryn had fetched tea from the kitchen area where Douglas kept a woodburning cookstove going on cold days. The house was exceptionally well insulated. It had solar panels and a battery storage system for light at night, and a small water powered generator in a stream nearby. But the stream flow had been reduced during the dry summer making it quick to freeze, so the solar panels were the primary source of electricity now. They weren't going to be helping much on this grey today. Fortunately, the water generator could still power one or two LEDs for night work, but not much more.

Kathryn handed Redd a cup of tea, and they took seats and watched Douglas pull the threads through the holes to build an illustration.

"How large are you going to make this one?" asked Redd. "I guess there's a limit since you have to reach under to make the stitch."

"Well, some people up in Canada made one that was the size of a rug, I think fourteen or fifteen feet by twenty-four feet long. Millions of stitches. Not my thing. I'm not sure how they did it. Rolled up the part they had finished, I guess. What's the deal with your missing con men?"

"The wife—she's also the kid's mother—thinks it has something to do with Native American art, her son trying to sell it in Europe? But the son is a novice and doesn't even have a gallery here. I just started on it yesterday, but it doesn't make sense."

"Art scams take a long time to develop and perfect. One of the investors in the company I worked for got taken. Fakes. Very good ones I guess, but fakes. Modern stuff. He should have asked me."

"I didn't know you were an expert on art fakes," said Kathryn.

"I'm not, but logic and the odds should have told him they were extremely unlikely to be real."

"I don't think we're dealing with anything at that level," said Redd. "It may not involve art fraud at all. I have no idea. But I would like to at least figure out where their current money is coming from and also try to figure out where they are. I need to get into their credit card records."

"I thought the FBI did all that stuff."

"They won't be able to go deep enough."

"Okay, I'll come over in a day or two and see what I can find."

Douglas was concentrating on a section with a dozen or more different colored dots and was probably ready for them to leave by now. He loved his sister and liked Redd, but he loved being alone more. Redd and Kathryn said goodbye and left with a nod from Douglas.

15

Scandals

Redd found a file from Berry when he and Kathryn got back to the house. It provided some detail on Tom McFerren. He had moved around the country as various scandals followed him. He and a group of investors had tried their hands at the private equity fund approach, buying businesses and loading them with debt and cashing out. They had not had the size or expertise to pull it off, and the fund had crashed. They had been fined and sanctioned by the court, but no one went to prison.

McFerren himself had invested in a warehouse in Richmond. It had burned under suspicious circumstances with an inventory of supposedly industrial plastic feed stock stored there. The investigation showed that the volume of material stored there was misrepresented and of a lower quality, or possibly almost valueless, recycled material bundled for export. In the end, the insurance company had paid out a small amount. McFerren was suing for more.

There were five separate bankruptcies involving commercial and industrial buildings in various cities. He had been part of a failed bank in New Mexico and had invested in a chain of high-interest loan facilities. It seemed he had no idea how to do business honestly, which led Redd to believe that whatever he was involved with now was equally illegal.

There were no references to offshore accounts. Redd would need Douglas to ferret that out, if he could.

16

At Any Rate

It was nearly five o'clock when Redd's cell phone rang and showed the number of a competent attorney he knew of from Charlottesville, Lawrence Luther. Luther had a reputation for being thorough and tough. He won cases. Redd had never had a case before him but had seen him in action in several trials and respected him.

"Mr. Herring? Lawrence Luther, good afternoon."

"Lawrence, good afternoon. What can I do for you? I haven't been in court for a while. I assume all is well with you?"

"Yes, all well and normal. But I do have something that has come up. Do you know an attorney over here by the name of Gabriel Dunbar?"

"No, I don't think so. Criminal or civil work?"

"Criminal primarily. At any rate, he's heard of you, and asked specifically about you. You've been involved in some high-profile cases recently."

"Not that I wanted to be. Where is this leading?"

"Ah, straight to the point. I'd like to hire you to do some investigative work, if I could."

"Wrong person, I'm afraid. I'm only doing work on call for the FBI right now."

"That's what I was afraid of, but hear me out. This is something really, really out of the ordinary, and it doesn't make sense."

"It won't matter, but tell me."

"Here's the deal, as explained by Gabe to me. His wife was going to be out of town, and he arranged secretly for a friend of hers that he had known for years to stay in their guestroom for a couple of days, and he screwed her. Why he didn't just put her up at a hotel, I have no idea. But at any rate, they have sex the first night, and on the next morning she's nowhere to be found. Clothes still there in the guestroom, toiletries, the whole works."

"I'll admit that's strange."

"Well, it gets stranger. Dunbar's wife calls and says she's coming home two days early, the same day the friend goes missing. Gabe flips out and hastily tries to remove evidence that the missing friend has been there and leaves the house. The wife gets home and finds some blood in the basement."

"Oh geez."

"She calls the cops. They determine its human blood and look around the house some more and find a dirty towel upstairs and another bloody cloth. Gabe had washed the sheets but forgot the pillowcases, and had made the bed sloppily."

"So he's caught now."

"And how. So, anyway, down at the station, where they take them both, they quickly determine the wife was out of town, just got back an hour before she called the cops, and has an alibi for the night before and that morning. But the guy was off in the hills somewhere and his clothes have dirt on them. He's wearing a suit. They take his car in, his SUV, and find some woman's hair in the trunk space and on the passenger seat. They trace where he was on his cell phone and are off looking in the mountains to see if he hid something or left a body there."

"What's his story?"

"He finally admitted that the woman, Sandy something, was there, they had sex, she disappeared, he has no idea where she went, and claims she left with all of her clothes and stuff this morning when he was asleep. His phone does show him trying to text or call her."

"But, no body has been found?"

"No, but the cops tried to call the woman, whose name is Sandy Wellsley, and got no response. They got the police in Sacramento, California, where she lives, to go by her apartment, and she wasn't there, and no one had seen her for about a week. She's divorced and moved there only six weeks or so ago, so doesn't really know anyone in the area well anyway."

Redd thought about what he had just heard from Lawrence. "How well do you know this guy, Gabe? What's his reputation?"

"He's pretty proud of himself, but not a sociopath. I've played golf with him. He's a good golfer and may cheat a bit on the green, but an overall okay person. Not capable of killing someone. Well, I guess most everyone's capable of murder under the right circumstances, but I don't see this."

"Go back for a minute. You said the wife came back from out of town unexpectedly?"

"Yeah, the uncle she was visiting got sick, I guess."

"Weird. Is it possible someone other than Gabe came in and killed her and took her away?" asked Redd.

"It doesn't seem possible. I mean, anything is possible, but it would have had to have been the first night, and Gabe said he might have heard a door close, but no big activity."

"Could she have snuck out? I mean, she must have. But why? Did she set this guy up?"

"It looks like it, but what's the motive? Gabe says he can't think of one. And where would she have gone?"

"I don't think I've ever encountered anything like this before. Where do things stand right now? Is he out on bail?"

"He hasn't been charged with anything yet. The wife kicked him out. He's in a hotel."

"Well, he's in a world of trouble even if he's not guilty of killing the woman," said Redd.

"Tell me. So, can you help us? It will pay well."

"I don't know." said Redd. "Let me think about it. It's certainly unusual. I'll get back to you tomorrow. I need to clear it with my FBI person if I decide I'm interested. Let me know if anything new comes up."

"I appreciate your time and you considering it. I hope you say yes. This guy is not one of my favorite people, but he's not a killer."

17

A New Twist

Redd told Kathryn about the call and the conversation with Lawrence at dinner. She listened intently and then thought about it before speaking.

"It has to be the woman, Sandy, who set this up, don't you think? Unless he really did kill her."

"That's what I think, too. They need to look for a motive, for her I mean. What did he do to hurt her or her family?"

"You said she's divorced. Did he play a part in that?"

"No idea, that wasn't mentioned. But, it just got started, so maybe we'll learn something in the next day or so. I don't know who they will have investigate it. There are some competent people on their team there."

"Can you have a murder charge without a body?"

"You can, but getting a conviction is almost impossible without overwhelming evidence in some form. Like massive bloods stains in the killer's car, or in the house, the presence of a weapon, witness statements, and so on. In a lot of cases the killer eventually confesses or someone turns him or her in, so finding the body matters less."

"Are you going to help with this?"

"I don't know. It's intriguing. He's acting guilty, but it all seems a bit haphazard and unplanned. I'd think if you were planning to kill someone, you'd think ahead. Maybe not, unless it was a crime of passion."

"When will you decide?"

"Do you think I should look into it?" he asked Kathryn.

"You see things other people don't, and you believe in justice, sometimes uniquely. I think it suits you as far as complexity. But it's up to you. Things always happen in pairs for you, don't they?"

"Lately it seems like it. I'll sleep on it."

Redd helped Kathryn fill the dishwasher and was headed to the office to check emails when his phone rang. It was Lawrence.

"A new twist," he said before Redd could even say anything. "The cops found a note in some papers on Gabe's desk asking for a hundred thousand dollars to keep quiet."

"What?" replied Redd.

"A note supposedly from Sandy to Gabe asking for a hundred thousand to not tell his wife. They've picked him up at his hotel and booked him for suspicion of murder."

"And what does he say?"

"He's never seen the note. But the cops are still trying to figure out why he went to the mountains. His phone shows his route, and he stopped up there, but it snowed a bit in the mountains, and there are no tracks, and they haven't found a body or anything else yet."

"What's next?"

"We will offer to post bail and see if the judge accepts it. This is certainly a bad development, but it doesn't make any more sense than any of the rest of it."

"Yeah, why wouldn't she just ask him for it?"

"I don't know. Maybe she did, and he refused, and she wrote this to remind him—or could use it to show the wife. I have no idea."

"Alright, I'll get back to you tomorrow. Good night." Redd went back into the kitchen and told Kathryn about the call and the note.

"Weird," was all she said.

18

Shotgun

Marta Miller missed a violent death or worse by five minutes. She had left the house feeling a bit queasy that morning, probably from the last glass or two of Chardonnay from the night before. She had run out of the good stuff and opened a bottle that someone had left that was too sweet, but it had had to do. There were plenty of reds there, but they were too heavy and too dry.

She would normally have turned to the right out of the driveway and gone to the connection with the interstate, south to Roanoke or north toward Staunton for the connection to Charlottesville where there were plenty of options for food and wine and a nice lunch. But today, she turned left on the county road, because she wanted to check to make sure the gate to a field behind the house, on the east side, was locked so that hunters and four-wheelers couldn't get in. Tom had had the gate installed the previous autumn. She would normally have left the checking to him or Nathan, when he was there. But being alone in the house, she worried that someone might come in that way and come up to the house from the back at night.

There was a turn-in at the gate, and she pulled in, just as a wave of nausea hit her. She quickly got out of her suburban and leaned over just in time. She was in the middle of the second wave of throwing up when she heard the white noise of a vehicle coming from the direction of the interstate. The noise level dropped, and it registered with her that the vehicle was turning into the driveway to her house. Strange.

She threw up one more time, and that seemed to be it. She wiped the sour taste from her mouth with a Kleenex from a packet in the car just as she heard shots up at the house that sounded like those from a shotgun. At first she thought she should head back to the house to see what was happening, but then it occurred to her that no hunters would be that close, and there would be no game to be hunted with shotguns up there.

She thought she heard voices, and then the sound of more shots and maybe breaking glass. What were they doing, shooting out the doors and windows? She had been startled by the car noise, then frightened by the first shots, and now she was terrified. She jumped back in the car and backed onto the road and headed further east and away from her driveway, hoping that whoever was at the house had not heard her car leave.

Marta was in luck, because the winds from the west that had carried the sound of the approaching vehicle and the shots to her, had also carried the sound of her Suburban away to the east and away from the two men dressed in hunter camouflage who had shot in the doors to the house and were now looking through the rooms for an inhabitant.

19

Me or the Guys?

Redd got the call from Marta ten minutes after she pulled away from the back gate. There was no cell signal toward the mountain, and she had to make three turns to get to a road that would get back to the interstate or to old Route 11 where her phone would work. She gave him a quick and disjointed description of what she had heard. From her description of location, the closest police department would be in Buena Vista. He told her to drive straight there, park in back and go in and report what had happened. He would alert the county officers and would head to her house immediately.

For a minute he missed having his sheriff vehicle with its siren and flashing light that allowed him to move along the highway at top speeds. But he had a magnetic temporary flasher, and he popped it onto the cab of his pickup and headed toward Marta's house as quickly as was safe. It took him over thirty minutes to get there, and he found the property surrounded by state police and local deputies. The shooters had left, but the front door had been shot through as well as some of the first-floor French doors. They had apparently been looking for her or her husband and son, because the house showed no signs of a search for papers or valuables or any other item. They must have conducted the search quickly and gotten out of there fast. Otherwise, they would have run into sheriffs' vehicles coming from several directions. Redd initially thought of the traffic cams on the interstates, but they had no idea what type of vehicle they might be looking for.

The shooters had picked up the shells from the shotguns and the paved driveway left no prints from tires. The house had a security system, but Marta had forgotten to set it when she left that morning. It would most likely not have frightened away these men anyway, they had been so intent on getting into the house.

It would not be safe for Marta to stay there now. The shooters might well come back, and the local police forces could not provide 24-hour protection. And the doors would need to be repaired immediately or boarded up. It was already getting cold in the house.

Two deputies were assigned to watch the house, and Redd drove to Buena Vista to meet with Marta. She described the events of the morning as clearly as she could.

"What do you think they were after?" she asked. "Me or the guys?"

"Probably information," said Redd. "I'm guessing your son, at least, has something of theirs, and they want to know where it got to."

"That's a pretty violent way to find out, don't you think?" responded Marta. "Whatever it is must be really valuable."

"I would say so," said Redd, "and I don't think its framed Native America artwork."

Marta was silent for a moment. "No, that wouldn't make sense."

"No. Do you have any sense of what they might have been up to? Truthfully, I mean you didn't really tell me much the other day."

"Sheriff, I told you all I know, honestly. I don't know what Nathan was doing. I really did think he was doing something with art selling."

"I know you said that, but he doesn't appear to have an art gallery, so something else is at play, and it looks as if he is playing with very dangerous people."

"I realize that now, Sheriff, and I don't know what to tell you, and I don't know what I'm going to do. I can't go back there to that house. What am I going to do? I'm afraid to go to a hotel. What if they track me?"

"I agree you can't go back there. And, Ma'am? I'm not the sheriff."

"I need someone like you to protect me," she said, more coyly than Redd would have anticipated given the gravity of the situation. He wondered if she realized how close she had come to being kidnapped or raped or killed. Or tortured. Or all four.

"We'll help you figure out something. I'll get in touch with some folks. In the meantime, we need to see to getting your house sealed up where they broke in. Do you have a handyman or repair service, or does your husband do all that?"

"No way in hell. He doesn't know a wheelbarrow from a lawn mower. I have someone I can call."

Redd left her to make her call—or calls—and it was arranged for a deputy to take her back to the house and get clothes and personal items enough to hold her for several weeks. He called Berry and told him what had happened and asked about a safe house. Berry had nothing he could offer. Redd decided that the large hotel in Staunton should be safe enough for her for a few days, and there was another option that might make sense, but he needed to think that through and see if it would be practical.

20

Getting the Locks Changed

Celia Dunbar was one furious woman. She was most furious about the fact that he had screwed Sandy in their home as opposed to off in some hotel. She would be the object of derision and humor on social media, which she hated almost more than the betrayal. And the doubly humiliating scandal of a murder charge? What a moron her husband was.

The police had finally finished with all of the fingerprinting and sample-taking and whatever else the hell they had to do, and she had immediately called her cleaning lady and told her she'd pay her double-time—hell, triple-time—to come over and clean the place from top to bottom and to pack up her husband's clothes and put them on the front porch where he could come and get them. She was also getting the locks changed.

Alice Monroe had been cleaning for the Dunbar's for five years and liked Gabriel better than she liked Celia, neither of them being salt-of-the-earth kind of people. Neither had much appreciation for the delivery people, the waiters and waitresses, or folks like the lawn mowing guy and the window cleaners and the house cleaner, of course. But Gabe was a bit friendly, and they did give her a decent Christmas bonus, so she talked Celia into letting her at least put his clothes on the back porch where they wouldn't get wet and ruined. Bail had been granted to Gabe based on his standing as an attorney. He was at the Boar's Head in a suite, but he didn't have the income to sustain that for long. Especially since he was not likely to have a house to live in for some time, and a host of legal bills would soon be headed his way.

Gabe had readily admitted his guilt with Sandy, but claimed he had been drinking and not thinking straight, which was worse to Celia than just admitting he was as much the driver as was Sandy. To her credit, Celia was finding it hard to believe that he had killed Sandy. She knew from social media that Sandy, who she also knew from college days, was recently divorced and that she had suffered losses in her family fairly steadily over the years. But that was not Celia's fault. And if Sandy couldn't manage her own life and affairs, it was not Celia's problem and wasn't Gabe's either. She thought that if the request for money, the blackmailing, was true, then Sandy was at a worse place in her life than was apparent from social media. But it still wasn't forgivable. Not cause for murder. And she thought she would have seen something in Gabe's behavior at some time during their marriage that would have revealed a tiny streak of potential for such violence. Maybe not. Maybe under the right circumstances a person could just snap.

21

Illegal Drugs?

Late in the afternoon of the attack at Marta's house, Redd called Berry again and gave him an update. He had installed Marta at the hotel and told her to be cautious. Staunton police would keep an eye out, but that was going to be difficult with Staunton being at the intersection of two interstates and two sets of exits with all of the usual fast food, cheap motel, and gas station chains. Most of the travelers never made it to downtown, but any extra vigilance was of some value, Redd hoped.

"I guess you still have no clue as to what these two marauders were up to?" asked Berry.

"No, but they're obviously out for someone around here. What does that imply to you?"

"I think one of two things. The kid either stole something or he's a courier."

"Courier for what? Illegal drugs? Who'd be smuggling drugs from the US to Europe? That's double the risk," said Redd. "I don't see that at all."

"What about the art stuff? Have you seen what he was supposedly selling?"

"Not yet. Remember I just got pulled into this two days ago and have nothing but the Miller woman's story to go on so far. The attack on the house means there's something going on that's bigger than it first appeared, but I'm just getting started."

"See if you can find out what he's selling, and then maybe we can see if we have anything that will help you. Call me when you have something." Berry hung up.

Redd was frustrated by the lack of anything substantial to go on. Berry had asked him to look into the case, but so far he didn't have much more than he could have gleaned from a decent internet search. He decided that in the morning he would take Marta with him to her son's apartment in Charlottesville to see what could be learned there. He had still not made up his mind about looking into the disappearance of the woman who had screwed the attorney. That was also strange. What was the deal with all of these people disappearing?

He called Marta on her cell phone to ask her for more information on exactly what type of products her son was supposedly selling. She answered right away.

"Marta, I think it would be a good idea to go to your son's apartment tomorrow morning and see what we can find there. Probably should have started with that."

"Yes, of course, I have keys. Will you be taking me?"

"Yes," said Redd, ignoring the wordplay. "I'll pick you up at 8:30 tomorrow morning. Does your son have a studio or any kind of work area attached to his apartment, or as a part of it? Does he work from home?"

"I think he has some sort of work area, but I haven't paid that much attention. Why?"

"Well, I'm just trying to figure out what he has or had that bought on this attack which is undoubtedly linked to his disappearance."

"Of course. I see."

"So, unless he was making it up, supposedly something related to the art business must be the key to his disappearance. And it would be nice to know what the intruders wanted at your place today. I wonder how they knew where you live?"

"I have no idea. Don't you think I'd tell you if I did? This is terrifying."

"Yes, I'm sure you would have. I just hope tomorrow sheds some light on this. Is his apartment in a complex or is it a standalone building?"

"It's in one of those old historic buildings—a loft I think he calls it. He wanted somewhere secure."

"Alright, we will see what we see in the morning. You haven't had any issues at the hotel, I take it?"

"None that companionship wouldn't cure."

"Goodbye, Mrs. Miller," said Redd, pointedly emphasizing the Mrs. He wondered if he should have someone else go with them to Charlottesville in the morning.

22

Scammers

Marta was waiting for him in the lobby at 8:30 when he arrived. She was dressed in tight jeans, sensible but stylish sneakers, a cashmere sweater over a silky blouse. She pulled on a long classic wool coat and wrapped a designer scarf around her neck before going out into the cold to get in the truck cab. He opened the door for her, and she held onto his hand for longer than needed as he helped her get in. It was going to be a long day.

They reiterated a few points from the conversation the evening before, but Marta seemed bored by it. "Why don't you tell me about yourself," she said to Redd. "I looked up some news stories about you last night, online. You are quite famous around here."

"You know all there is to know then," said Redd. "I just happened to get involved in some complex issues of late."

"That's not all you got involved in I see. I looked up your girlfriend. Wow, she's pretty hot. And I guess damn smart. And gotta be rich with all those cattle and farms and so on."

"Let's leave her out of this, if you don't mind."

She laughed. "You're funny. I'd like to meet her."

"I'm sure she'd love to meet you, too."

"Don't be patronizing. Don't you think I'm good enough to meet her?"

"I didn't say or imply that. I can only assume you are good enough to meet anyone. I've had too many cases come too close to home, and I'd like to keep my personal world and my investigation worlds in separate boxes."

"So, all we have in common is you."

Redd was beginning to be irritated. "No, you don't have me in common. Do you have any idea what could have happened to you yesterday, or do you know something about the intruders you aren't telling me about? You could be dead right now, or worse."

"What's worse than dead?" She paused. "No, you're right. There are things. I apologize. I'll shut up for a bit. And I don't and didn't know who the intruders were." She turned to look out the window as they crossed the mountain and didn't speak again until they were exiting the interstate at Charlottesville when she needed to give Redd directions to the apartment.

The building had a plaque out front stating that it was over one hundred years old. It had been a warehouse of some sort and had been converted to high-end apartments. Nathan's was on the top floor. There was no doorman, but a security code had to be entered to access the lobby, and a sign warned against letting strangers in. The elevator also required a coded card, much like higher-end hotels. Marta had the codes and a key to the apartment.

The unit itself was large and bright with a high, industrial-style ceiling. Supporting joists and cleaned and stained timbers contributed to the upscale statement of the building. There were two bedrooms. The first was a normal bedroom with a queen-sized bed, modern dresser, and nightstands holding lamps with sturdy glass bases. There were a few art prints on the walls. Redd didn't recognize the artists, but that was no surprise. Marta had remained mostly silent since the exchange in the truck and was looking closely at the prints.

"These are very high quality giclées," she said.

"I've heard Kathryn mention that term," Redd replied, "but I'm not sure I understand it."

"It's a more expensive printing process that makes the underlying piece look more like the real thing. Lots of artists hate it. But a few others make some money off it."

"How do you know about this?" he asked her.

"Nathan explained it. I haven't been in here for a while. I didn't know he had these. There isn't much room to display stuff in the apartment overall, with the larger windows." Indeed, there had been nothing of note in the way of art in the living room, just some wall hangings and a few Pier 1-type terracotta-looking statuettes on several tables.

They left the first bedroom and opened the door to the second. The room was completely dark, with both room-darkening curtains and several panels over the windows to block out all light. It was essentially a darkroom.

In the center of the room was a heavy-looking table, made of several layers of butcher block. It was supported on sturdy oak legs and had what looked like a sheet of steel on top. Mounted on a tripod made of heavy steel legs was a standard camera, a Nikon single lens reflex.

"Ah," said Marta. "He told me he was going to set something up to do giclée. Now I understand."

"What does this have to do with it?" asked Redd.

"You need a very clear photo to work from to get the printer to make a good giclée. There can be no shadow, no sheen from any light and no movement. This camera is probably on a timer, and he would set it and leave the room, so as not to jiggle anything. This warehouse is perfect with its huge beams and foundation. Very clever."

"And then what?"

"He must have a very good giclée printer somewhere, or else someone unethical is printing for him, which would mean he's marketing unauthorized prints."

"Is there that much of a market for this?"

"That's the catch. I don't think you could get rich at it. It's not worth the risk, I wouldn't think."

"You seem to know more than you were letting on," said Redd. "What haven't you told me?"

"It's not that big a deal. I worked in a couple of galleries here and there. I was never an expert. I just repeated what the owner told me to say. Flirted with the male patrons. That sort of thing. But I do know a little about the techniques and margins. I don't know. There has to be more."

"And you don't know where he might have the printer? Does he frame them?"

"That's usually done by a specialist. That's a skill all its own. But he was talking about selling them framed. I assume he would have someone make the frames for him."

They had turned on one light and now turned on more. There was a cabinet with trays, and when Redd pulled out the drawers, he could see that they contained larger prints of works by a range of artists.

Redd decided that it would make the most sense to take photographs of the prints with the artists names and print titles and to either research the names himself or give them to someone with direct knowledge. He could also have the FBI check to see if there was a record of fraud surrounding the marketing of these artists.

23

Charlottesville

While Redd was taking photos of the artists' names and the titles of their work, he asked Marta to look through the drawers and a desk in the master bedroom to see if she could find any references to travel plans, contacts, phone numbers, or a printer or frame maker.

Nathan did not appear to be overly organized. While the apartment was generally neat and in good order except for where dust had settled on surfaces during his absence, the papers in his desk drawers were jumbled and in no order.

Marta did not find utility bills or credit card bills, but assumed those must have been online. No bank statements, which could also have been online.

There was no monitor for a computer anywhere in the apartment so she assumed that he must only use a laptop. At the bottom of the right-hand drawer, she found one, something like a little MacBook, tucked under a pile of loose papers and art show fliers. She called to Redd and told him what she had found. He told her to bag up everything in the drawers and they would take it all back to the hotel or his house to go through it. In a kitchen drawer she found the charger for the computer and its cords. But she had so far not found any usernames or passwords.

While Redd was in the middle of taking photos, his phone buzzed, and the caller was Lawrence.

"Redd, Lawrence here. I wonder if you've had time to think about our proposal? Or request?"

Redd had been on the fence and had been so involved with Marta's issues that he hadn't thought it through yet. "I'm tied up with another problem right now, another missing person case, as it turns out, but why don't I meet your client in person and decide based on that interview. Does that work for you?"

"Of course. When can we meet? He is obviously available at any time."

"I am, just coincidentally, in town right now, down in the old town section."

"Oh, that's great. Can we meet today then?"

"I've got a client with me, so can we park her somewhere? She's under my protection right now."

"Really. Well, sure. She can hang out here at the office, or we can meet Gabe at the Boar's Head, and she can wait for us in the lobby or lounge. Does that work?"

"Either is safe, I'm sure. Let's meet at your office. If you have a spare conference room, I'll put her to work sorting some papers we just found. You are out on Barrack's Road?"

"No, but just up from there. I'll text the address, and you can put it in your phone. And I'll reserve a conference room for your client. We are west of the main campus on old 250. In an hour?"

"Sure, we can grab a bite in the meantime."

Redd clicked off and told Marta what the new plan was.

24

Tight Jeans

There were various food options at street level, and they chose one that had a quick lunch service with soup and salad or sandwich. Marta had found several empty grocery bags and had put all of the papers she could find into them, and Redd had the computer and the cords. He would have Douglas work on access to the computer files.

Redd explained the schedule for the next few hours, and she was happy with it. He had to admit that she was a very attractive and sexy woman. She had irritated him on the drive over, but all of their conversations since then had been polite and professional. During lunch he could detect a slight smile on her face and wondered what she was thinking about. She had taken off her coat and sat up straight in her chair, a position that highlighted her cleavage across the table from him. When she walked to the restroom, it was hard not to appreciate the look of her body in tight jeans.

After lunch they drove to the law offices. They took the bags of papers and the laptop in with them. A receptionist had been told to expect them, and Lawrence was summoned right away. He looked with admiration and a bit more at Marta, and then showed her to a small conference room two doors down on the left. He asked the receptionist to offer her coffee or water, and then they left her to her work on the papers.

Lawrence spoke to Redd on the way to his office. "You didn't tell me you had such a hot client. She's obviously not the one missing. Not missing anything. Who's gone? Surely not her husband?"

Redd chuckled. "She is a handful, excuse the expression." Lawrence laughed. "It's quite serious. Her son and husband are both missing in Europe, and there was a break-in at her house when she had just pulled away. We don't know what's going on."

"Oh yeah, there was a spot on the news last night about someone shooting out some doors or windows over by Lexington. Is that the case?"

"Yeah, that's it. Could have been a lot nastier. Anyway, let's meet your client and see what he has to say for himself. Too many missing people."

"Sure, he should be here in about five minutes."

At that, Lawrence's landline rang, and it was the receptionist announcing Gabe's arrival. She showed him back to Lawrence's office.

25

It Was Late

After introductions, Redd asked Gabe to tell him, in as much detail as possible, what had happened. Redd made notes of the key points and stopped Gabe from time to time to clarify a timeline or specific item.

When they got to the point that the note asking for money had been found, Redd stopped Gabe. "I want to get this clear. You say you had never seen the note, and she never asked you for money while she was with you?"

"No, we didn't really talk about much of anything serious. And we didn't talk about money."

"I understand that she was divorced. Is that right? And recently?"

"Yes, I think so. I'm almost certain."

"And you didn't discuss that, what caused it, anything like that?"

"Just briefly. She said she didn't really want to discuss it. She said they had grown apart and he was boring and she wanted out."

"Nothing else?"

"Not really. They never had kids, so that wasn't a subject to be dealt with."

"Where did they live before the divorce?"

"San Francisco, I think, or around there."

"And I think Lawrence here told me she was now living in Sacramento. Is that right?"

"Yeah," said Gabe.

"Did you talk about what she was doing there? Job? Where she was living? Friends?"

"We talked about it a little. Listen, I know this sounds bad, especially with her disappearing and all that, but honestly, I was mostly thinking about whether I was going to get her into bed, and I wasn't paying close attention to the other stuff. She was sitting in a kind of teasing pose, you know, with her dress riding up and all, and I was just thinking about sex. Sorry. I figured we had a couple of days to catch up on other things."

"How long had you known her? Where did you meet?" asked Redd.

"A few years. We met when I was in law school. She was undergrad, and we met at a party, but we were both with other people, and nothing happened but a little flirting."

"So, I'm confused," said Redd. "Is that the last time you saw her, in law school? How many years ago?"

"Sorry, I should have made that clear. She went to work as an administrative assistant for a tech firm on the west coast, and every now and then our firm handled some legal work for them on things here in Virginia. I ended up working with her after law school. That would be three or four years ago now."

"And you never had an affair with her during that time?"

"No, but I had a sense that she had followed my career and that it was maybe her influence that got our law firm involved in their intellectual property and copyright work here in the state. I'm almost sure of it, because otherwise they would have used a Richmond or northern Virginia firm."

"So why do you think she did that?" asked Lawrence, who had been following the Q&A session and not adding anything. "It sounds like she was keeping track of you. Did she have a reason for that? I mean she was married and a long way away."

Gabe paused and seemed about to say something, paused again, and then said, "I don't know. I can't think of anything."

Redd glanced at Lawrence. There was more there, but he wasn't going to try to coax it out at this point. He wanted more background first. He felt like Gabe was lying on several fronts, but wasn't sure what the motive would be. He was hoping the cops would turn up something more to go on.

"Does she have family around somewhere—mom, dad, brothers, sisters?" asked Redd.

"No, she had a sister who died a couple of years ago, and mom and dad died just after that. They weren't that old, but both had issues, I think. Health issues, I mean."

"So, you do know that."

"Yes, it was on social media—the parents, that is—and I knew about the sister from Sandy."

"What happened with the sister? Accident? Illness?"

"She killed herself," said Gabe and looked away.

No one spoke for a moment, and Redd looked at his notes. Then he spoke.

"So, what do you want me to do?" he asked Gabe. "It seems like you have background on the family."

"I'd really like for you to prove that I am innocent by finding her alive, wherever she is."

"That's what I thought. I'm not sure where to even start. She obviously didn't disappear into thin air, but that's how it looks. If we assume you didn't kill her, how do you account for her getting out of the house without you knowing? Are you that heavy a sleeper?"

"The only thing I can think of is that she put something in my drink. I don't know. We drank a lot, and it was late. I did think I heard a door close one time but then decided it was in a dream."

"Did you get up and walk around the house, check anything out?"

"No, I never really fully woke up. I guess she could have gone into my office and put the note there and gone to the basement and poured some blood from somewhere down the drain. I don't know where that blood or the blood on the towel came from."

"Your house wasn't alarmed?"

"I didn't have it turned on. I forgot."

"What about the doors? Wouldn't you have found one unlocked?"

"The front door has a deadbolt, but that wasn't engaged. The other lock, on the handle, can be set to lock when you pull it shut. She could have gone out that way, or out the back—that locks on its own, too. I didn't check that, didn't think to."

"Lawrence," said Redd, "I assume you have checked with the cab company to see if a taxi came to pick her up?"

"Yes, but they said no. And there aren't many ride services like Uber around here."

"I think I would have heard a car," said Gabe. "Or seen some lights."

"Maybe," said Redd. "If she didn't take a cab, how far would she have to walk to get some way out of town? The airport is a long way away. I assume you checked with the airlines?"

"The police did, and there was no record of her on any flight out that day."

"Could someone have picked her up? An accomplice, if we assume a conspiracy?"

"I suppose, but she had just flown in that day."

"So many dead ends," said Redd. Lawrence nodded.

"I'll see what I can do," Redd continued. "But this is strange. Lawrence, can you ask the local police to let me talk to them about the case and share whatever they are willing to?"

"Sure, whatever you need."

Redd stood up and shook hands with Gabe. Lawrence told Gabe to wait, and he accompanied Redd to the conference room where Marta had succeeded in arranging the papers in piles by category.

Marta smiled and stood up when the two men entered the room. "I found something that might help us," she said to Redd.

"Let's discuss it in the truck on the way back to Staunton. That's good news."

Lawrence thanked him for coming in and for the offer to help and showed them both out.

26

Grey Cinderblock Building

Marta couldn't wait to tell Redd what she had found. She started talking as they left the building and headed for the truck.

"Redd, I did find the name of a business, a printing business, it says."

"Where did you find this name? As a bill, a business card, or what?"

"Oh yes," she said, ignoring the detail of the question. "It's a company, right here in Charlottesville, of all things. Can we go by there?"

"Show me the address."

She pulled out a sheet that looked like a delivery receipt from a freight forwarding company. On the sheet were several items with various parts or serial numbers, but the largest item was a laser printer of some type. The receipt was from four months earlier, around the beginning of September.

The address was on Highway 29 south toward Lynchburg. Redd turned to the right from the law firm parking lot and then right again on old 29, and after three traffic lights was headed past the interstate intersection south. There were only scattered businesses out south, and they came to the freight company address within minutes. It was a grey cinderblock building with frosted glass windows and a small frosted glass pane in a heavy front steel door. There were bars over the windows and the front door. There was a larger side door for loading that did not have steel bars in front of it. There was no sign of life and no business sign on the building.

There was a gravel parking lot in front with oil stains here and there. The building had a large, padlocked steel grate which could swing open to allow access to the door.

"I don't suppose you found any keys back at the apartment, did you?" Redd asked.

"Afraid not."

"Normal bolt cutters won't cut that lock either. Let me see that delivery ticket."

She handed him the document, and he looked at it for a few moments. "I'm guessing this laser printer is used for that giclée process we discussed. He must have bought one and has it in the building there. But it's not that large. It would have fit in the apartment. I wonder why it's here and what else is in that building."

"Maybe that's his framing shop," said Marta.

"Could be, I suppose. I'll need to get a good acetylene torch and cut the lock off."

"Can you do it right away?"

"No, there's equipment at the farm, but I'll need to go and get it, and I'll need help. The tanks are heavy. We won't have time today."

"Crap."

"You didn't find anything else about this building, did you—a rental agreement, a deed, anything like that?"

"No. Maybe he has an office in the building."

"Maybe. Well, we'll find out tomorrow. We'll need to get a

locksmith to change out the door lock as well, unless we can come up with a key."

"There might be some of his keys at the house. I didn't think about that with the attack and all."

Redd gave her a puzzled look. "There also might be a key to the main lock, you know."

She smiled back sheepishly. "Of course, I'm sorry."

"Okay, don't worry. We can run by there on the way back to the hotel and see what you can find. Can you get into the house now, with it boarded up?"

"Yes. They didn't shoot out the back door, and I have my keys for that in my purse with the car keys."

"We will just have time before it gets too dark."

27

Awfully Complex

Marta fell asleep on the drive back from Charlottesville to her house. She went in the back way and found a key ring in a dresser in her son's room. There were keys of various sizes and kinds.

Redd opted not to go after the acetylene system, because he was fairly certain that these were all the keys they would need to get into Nathan's shop.

He was right. The next day he removed the lock from the steel gate and swung it back and unlocked three additional locks on the steel door, two deadbolts and one in the doorknob itself. This was a lot of security for such a nondescript building.

Once he and Marta were in, Redd turned on the overhead lights and closed the door and locked the doorknob and one of the deadbolts. He didn't mention to Marta that he had reached under the seat of his truck and picked up his pistol. He didn't know whether the men who had attacked her house were after her or not, or whether they would know about her current whereabouts, but if they knew enough to find her house, they could also probably locate Nathan's apartment and this building.

The building was much cleaner and neater on the inside than he had anticipated from the industrial exterior. The walls were lined with a kind of plastic-surfaced paneling, and the ceiling was the normal suspended type hung from wires, allowing the heating and cooking and electrical lines to run above. The building was warm, and a Modine heater could be heard pushing out warm air.

There was an office off to the rear, or at least an office-type area. The rest of the room contained several pieces of very sophisticated-looking machinery. One piece was a high-end laser printer. On the other side of the room there was a boxy machine that looked like a copier but turned out to be, on closer inspection, a large and very expensive 3-D printer. The third machine, further back, was a large-format laser cutter. On the tables around the machines there were printed metal, wood and plastic picture frames, and frame parts. It was all there in that spot except for the camera they had seen back in the apartment. Nathan could take a photo of a print and bring the chip with the information here to the printer and produce his own illegal giclées and then frame them with specially printed frames.

"I wonder why he wants to print the frames instead of buying them?" Redd asked Marta. "This seems awfully complex."

"I don't know. This is the first time I've seen this. I guess he can make the frames out of whatever material that machine can cut."

Redd noticed a door at the back. It opened into two other rooms that they hadn't seen. The doors were heavy and thick and unlocked. Inside he found another complicated set of tools, including a welder and smaller machines to cut and polish metal. The room was quite clean and had a metal-lined door at the back. Leaning against one wall were what looked like square metal tubes which Redd recognized as stock for welding the pieces of metal frames together. There were several sizes.

They would make unique and attractive frames for some of the prints that Nathan had photographed and would be a dramatic contrast for the Native American artwork. Even as a novice he could tell that much.

The metal-lined door led into another well-lit room that housed high-end scales and a metal table.

Marta had come into the room and was looking around. "Wow, this is quite a setup."

"And you've never been here?"

"No, I swear. I had no idea he was doing all of this."

"How long has he been doing it? You told me, but I forgot."

"A bit longer than I said earlier. I've thought about it. I think he told me he had begun to ship some stuff maybe a little less than six months ago. Tom and I had taken a cruise. I was actually pleased that he was doing something on his own and not working with his father so much."

Herring was baffled by the idea of this woman sticking with a con man, but maybe he had given her a good life. Strange.

"I suppose we need to load up all the files and paperwork we can find here and see what that tells us about what happened, or who he was meeting."

"Or maybe on his computer?" Marta said. "Did you look at it? I forgot to ask."

"No, I have someone who can do that. I'd be useless," he said.

Redd had the foresight to bring banker boxes in case they located anything they needed to take away. He had done searches and seizures in the past. There were five boxes of files and papers including the instruction manuals for the machines. They boxed all of it and took samples of the various picture frames as well. Redd would have to ask Roddy, his predecessor as county sheriff, if the sheriff's department could provide some temporary workspace to examine it all.

Marta and Redd chatted casually about their visits to Paris and London on the ride back to Staunton. Marta invited Redd to stay and have dinner with her at the casual restaurant in the hotel, but he declined.

28

Just As Bizarre

Redd dropped off Marta at the hotel and drove back to the farm, carrying the boxes and computer with him. He was pleased to see Douglas's pickup truck in Kathryn's driveway. Kathryn was home but about to go out to check on her cows. Redd asked her to wait a few minutes so he could change clothes and go with her. Douglas was in the kitchen making a bean and kale soup.

"How did your day go with the latest hottie on your client list?" Kathryn asked teasingly, as they drove over to the main barns.

"Give me a break," said Redd. "She's not really a client. I think it's her husband and son who are the clients—well, maybe. Anyway, she behaved pretty well."

"Did you find out anything useful?"

"We found a computer that Douglas can maybe get into and a bunch of files. It looks like the son was importing giclées into Europe, but probably counterfeits or copies of things he was not authorized to sell."

"Wouldn't the artists find out and sue him?"

"You would think so, but I imagine that unscrupulous dealers might look the other way. I don't know anything about the art market."

"So, what's your next step?"

"I hope the files and the computer will show us what he was shipping and where it went. He had gone to London and Amsterdam, so we can assume he's shipping there."

"How about the other case, the guy accused of murder with no corpse?"

"I met him today, at Lawrence's office. I don't know what to make of it." He gave her a brief rundown as they walked out into the pasture to look at the cows. "What he says seems believable, but he's hiding something, and no one can figure out where the woman went. Or why she left."

"It's pretty extreme to fake your death just to punish someone or get even with them."

"Well, there was some hesitation on his part about her family. I need to check into that. And about where she was living in Sacramento. I assume that no one has noticed that she hasn't returned."

"The Africans aren't back, are they?" Kathryn joked, referring to a recent case. "I suppose I shouldn't joke about that."

"No, you shouldn't, and they aren't. But this seems just as bizarre. There was human blood in the basement drain and blood on a towel. I forgot to ask if they checked the knives in the house. If there was blood it had to come from a cut or stabbing or some kind of wound. Everything in this case is a stretch. I'm beginning to think we had very ordinary criminals when I was sheriff. Nothing complicated, all easily caught. The good old days of crime."

Kathryn laughed. "You may be right. I saw a piece in the local paper online about a drive-by shooter being found asleep in his car with the guns in plain sight. That fits your definition of a simple bad guy. Makes Roddy's job easy. I wonder how he's doing now that he's the sheriff?"

"That reminds me, I need to call Roddy. I want to see if we can use some office space over there. And I haven't talked to him since before Christmas."

29

Value-Added Tax

After dinner, Douglas took Nathan's computer into Redd's office, and within an hour he was back with a report.

"Your guy is doing monthly shipments to a company in Amsterdam. The company is not owned by your man, Nathan, but by someone who is either a citizen or has a residence permit. That is a requirement in the Netherlands. I checked."

"What happens after the company gets the prints or whatever?"

"That is the more interesting part. The artwork is valued very low, several hundred dollars per piece, and there is an import value-added tax for artwork that is only six-and-a-half percent. Only France is lower at five percent. Greece is twenty-three percent or so. The distribution company is paying the tax, but I don't show any funds coming back to your missing man. There are no records of bank transfers back to him."

"You found a bank account for Nathan?"

"Yes, and he transfers money in from time to time, but that comes from his father."

"None of it makes sense."

"Weirder is that the company in Amsterdam also doesn't seem to be selling the paintings or prints. They have inflows that I can trace, but no revenue stream from selling artwork."

"And I assume from my limited knowledge that this isn't something a collector would have set up?" said Redd. "At least not for this stuff."

"No, I wouldn't think so," replied Douglas, "unless this is a front for some other type of artwork or object that isn't listed here."

"None of this explains where Nathan is or why he went missing, does it?"

"No, you need to talk to Interpol or the police in Amsterdam or go deal with it yourself. How's your Dutch?" laughed Douglas. "Actually, most of them speak English. You'd be okay."

"I'm not planning on going to Amsterdam just yet. Maybe I can get Wendell to get in touch with someone and give us a report. Amsterdam is a big diamond market, but I don't think Nathan would have been smuggling diamonds over from the US."

"I think there have been some human trafficking rings broken up there, and there is drug smuggling everywhere, so it could be anything."

"All the worse for me and this investigation. Did you find out anything about where the father's money is coming from?"

"Nothing useful. He has an account in the Bahamas, or accounts. I can't get into all of them yet. He's into Bitcoin, but, of course, no one can break into that, and I don't have his password and won't be able to get it. That's the value of Bitcoin for illicit money transfers."

"I understand how it works, but why it isn't regulated is beyond me," replied Redd. "This is all helpful, though. Can you send me the name of the import company in Amsterdam, and I'll get Berry to work on that end of it. How about London, anything there?"

"Not yet. I did find that the art market in London took a major hit after Brexit. It used to be the best place for importing because they didn't have a levy. Now they have one in place, plus you then have to pay the value-added tax to the EU. Maybe he just went to London to go to the theater."

"Another dead end. That's all I can digest for now. Will you be here for a few days?"

"No, I have to buy some basics tomorrow, then I'll head back. It's supposed to get quite cold for a few days. I'll email you what I found."

30

Not Just Tulips

The next morning Kathryn left early to check her cows on the way to work. She didn't need Redd's help, so he logged onto his computer and found the summaries from Douglas which he forwarded on to Berry at the FBI office. Douglas had already gone into town to shop.

At 8:00 he called Berry, who picked up immediately. "I see your computer whiz is helping you again. He's better than some of ours."

"He should be," said Redd. "He designed half of the systems out there."

"Yeah, so you've said. So, what do you want from me, now?"

"It would help if you could get the embassy, or the Dutch police, or Interpol, or whatever, to check on the company that received the artwork from Nathan and see if they know anything about him or his dad. He must have gone there, since the computer records show that's where the prints were shipped."

"It won't be the embassy. If this was national security, they might send someone over, but not for this. I'll get in touch with Interpol to coordinate with the Dutch. Amsterdam is kind of a crime haven. Diamonds, drugs, girls, what have you."

"So, not just tulips?"

"No, not just tulips. What else do you need?"

"You must be bored," said Redd. "You never offer extra help."

"I am bored. We're fighting for funding, as usual, and I hate having to justify what we do."

"I'll put in a good word for you. I'll let you get back to it."

Redd clicked off and called Marta who answered right away. "Good morning, Sheriff. Do you have some news for me?"

"Still not the sheriff. I've learned a bit, but I'd rather discuss it in person, and we need to look over the papers we collected."

"I don't want to piss you off like yesterday, but I'd rather discuss it in person as well."

Herring sighed. "I was hoping for a workspace over in the sheriff's department, but they have some sort of regional training going on. There's an office and small conference room out here at the farm. We can organize the material there. I can pick you up in about fifteen minutes."

"Whatever you say. Will I get to meet your girlfriend?"

"Probably not, she's teaching today."

"Too bad. You know I'm not stupid."

"I never thought you were."

"Your girlfriend and I might get along. I've traveled to a lot of places, and I know something about art and…"

Redd interrupted. "I'm sure you might, but right now the main thing is finding your husband and son and keeping you from getting kidnapped or killed. I like to keep my professional life separate from my personal life. I think I already said that. I'll see you in fifteen minutes."

"Right. I'll see you at the front door, Sheriff." She laughed as she hung up.

31

All Work and No Play

Marta was dressed in tight jeans again and had on a turtle-neck sweater stretched close around the chest. She had another designer scarf around her neck and was wearing a puffy jacket and thin, soft leather gloves. She had on heavier black lace-up shoes and looked more like she was headed out to ski than to go through company records. She was wearing a tobog-gan, and her hair was pulled back in a classic Parisian style. Two men standing by the front door had their eyes glued to her ass as she got into the truck. Redd did not come around to open her door this time.

"Good morning again, Sheriff." She said as she pulled the seatbelt across and wiggled into place. "I haven't been on a real farm in a long time."

"You live in the country down there by Lexington."

"Yeah, but that's not a real farm."

"Where did you live before you moved there? When did you move there, by the way?" Redd wanted to keep the conversation on neutral ground if he could. At least this woman kept her clothes on most of the time. When he had first met the wife of a suspect in the last case, she had been naked.

"We've only been there a few months. We lived in Miami for a while, but we were in Richmond before that. That was very dull. I liked Miami. I felt like I was in Cuba or somewhere exotic half the time. Those people know how to party."

"I wouldn't know. Can't go to Cuba these days. What was Tom doing in Miami?"

"One of his investment schemes. He wanted to do something called private equity, or a version of it. I know what it means. I don't know how you do it without a lot of money though. And he never seemed to have that type of people around him. Honestly, Sheriff, I always wondered how he made some of these things work. I don't know if he was actively a con man all the time, but I guess he was a con man at heart."

Redd thought for a moment. "And that didn't bother you?"

Marta laughed. "Again, honestly, Sheriff, or Redd—can I call you Redd?"

"Sure."

"Okay, Redd. Honestly, I didn't really give a shit after a point. I could have had another husband, other men, some of them a bit powerful. In fact, I do from time to time, but most of them were just another version of Tom, just another scumbag under the surface. So better the devil you know than the one you don't, as the saying goes. Tom was always good to me—getting a little on the side, I'm sure—but the lifestyle and travel were great. Until the last year, I guess. That's been a bit boring."

"After Miami, I would think living in the Virginia countryside would be a bit tame for a party girl like you," Redd teased her.

"Like you would know. We weren't there a lot. I think maybe Tom was hiding out a bit. He never said, just blew it off, but he was trying to stay away from a few folks, I think. Still, we went to New York and out to L.A. and to Europe and on a cruise for quite a while. Tom told me we were going to move somewhere exciting before too long, as soon as he got a new investment thing going. Honestly, I didn't really believe him."

"Where was Nathan all this time?"

"He worked with his dad in Miami for a while, and then he also seemed to want to back away from whatever they were up to. I think he was doing something with cryptocurrencies, he mentioned a fund, but then all that blew up with that one guy. I think some of the people he was working with lost a bunch. Maybe not his fault, but you know, blaming the messenger kind of thing."

Redd thought it went a lot further than blaming the messenger but didn't comment. He wondered if maybe all of the deal-making and shady business enterprises might finally have caught up with the McFerrens, son and father. In the legitimate world the broker might lose a client. In the money-laundering criminal world you were more likely to lose your life.

They had now reached the farm, and Marta was looking with keen interest as they approached. "Does your girlfriend live in that huge house up on the hill?" she asked.

"No, she has a smaller place. Her father and stepmom used to live there. She lets Mary Baldwin and JMU use it for guests when they have a conference or event."

"Sweet," said Marta, meaning it in the new, hip way, not the pejorative one. "And you live with her?"

"Yes. It suits us," said Redd.

"I bet it does," said Marta. "Doesn't she have a spare bedroom? I'd be a lot safer under your protection out here, wouldn't I?" she laughed.

"You might be, but I wouldn't," replied Redd, with a slight frown. "You know, there's no one up at the big house today, we could work up there, and it's got better internet if we need it. You just have to promise to behave."

"I'll do my best," she said, as they turned into the drive and Redd got out to unlock a gate. There had been an incident with local rednecks a few cases back, and Redd and Kathryn had had to increase the security for the house.

Redd and Marta carried the boxes of records inside and put them on the floor by a large sturdy dining table that Kathryn had put in when they decided to let the colleges use the house. At one point they thought they would operate the house as an inn or bed and breakfast, but that venture got off to a rough start when some guests were murdered at a local event. A person who believed in ghosts might think the house was cursed.

Marta went to the large windows overlooking the barns and some of the pastures and looked out at the view below her. "Is that a landing strip down there?" she asked. "Does your girlfriend have a plane?"

"Yes, it's a landing strip, but she doesn't have a plane. Her father did, and some of her customers do."

"Holy crap. I should switch teams and go after your girlfriend. I'll sign up for one of her courses at UVA."

Redd shook his head. "Can we get to work? We have a lot to get through here."

Marta turned back from the window and pulled off her outer coat and threw it on a sofa.

"Yeah, yeah, all work and no play. Let's see what Nathan was up to."

32

English Tradition Stuff

They arranged the papers according to categories but did not find much of use. There were documents regarding the purchase of the machines and instruction manuals printed from the manufacturer's internet sites. It looked like the more useful information must be on the laptop that Douglas had been working with. And so far, other than finding the recipient of the bogus artwork in Amsterdam, there was nothing to show who Nathan or his dad had been working with.

They went through the materials from the large desk drawers and a small file cabinet first. There were still two boxes from smaller drawers and a box from a shelf by the door to the welding room. That box contained orders for welding supplies and delivery tickets for some expensive and exotic wood and for stainless steel. Nothing unusual.

"You know," said Marta, after a few more minutes of shuffling through the material, "when we were on a cruise on one of those little kind of luxury ships, you know, the kind that only hold a couple hundred people and you have your own butler and all…"

"No, I don't know," said Redd, "but go ahead."

"Well, we went on one of those last year. We started down in Southampton where all the ships used to stop when they had the Atlantic crossings. Anyway, we went from Southampton over to Iceland, to Reykjavik, and we stopped at a bunch of charming English places along the way, and Edinburgh, and those islands up there and so on. And there were tours into town when you stopped, the way they do. I went on most of those, but Tom, on a couple of days, didn't want to go, so he would stay on the ship, or he said he did. But I know he got off at a couple of places, and I think he was meeting someone."

"But you don't know who, or whether there really was anyone, or what was discussed?"

"No idea."

"And this was Tom, your husband? Not your son."

"Right. But I still think that whatever they were doing they were doing together, and that's the key thing."

Redd shook his head. "That could mean anything or nothing. Had Tom done business in England before?"

"I don't know for sure. I think he wanted to do something with horses for a while, but nothing came of that. He always had ideas about being this high-class acting gentleman farmer. He ate up that stuffy English tradition stuff. That's why he bought that damn house out there."

"So how does that help us right now?"

"I'm just saying, look for anything that might have an English connection. Nathan went to London first for some reason. His credit card record showed that much. Maybe there's a business card or something in all of this."

"I would think it would have shown up by now. But let's keep looking."

They continued, but came up with nothing from Nathan's print shop. "How thoroughly did you look through the stuff at his apartment?" Redd asked Marta. "Did you look closely at everything?"

She looked at Redd a bit sheepishly. "I don't know. Once I found the computer at the bottom of the drawer, I kinda thought we had all we needed. I don't recall anything English, but I can't guarantee it."

"Then we need to go back over there."

"I'm sorry, I should have looked more thoroughly."

"Never mind, let's box this back up and put it in the office here, and we can head back and get some lunch as well."

An hour later they were back in the apartment. They boxed up the contents of the desk as well as the items in the bedside table, and Redd looked through all of the toiletries in the bathroom. He didn't expect to find a stash of diamonds or drugs or coded messages, but it was strange that Nathan had kept the identities of the people he was meeting so secretive. Redd wondered who he was hiding those identities from. If he were selling national secrets, he would surely have a reason for stealth. But these were just fake pieces of artwork.

They stopped at a trendy vegetarian restaurant for lunch, and Marta had a glass of Pinot Gris with her kale and beet salad. Redd had sparkling water with a quinoa-based salad with citrus and avocado and a pistachio dressing. Marta had an espresso afterward, and Redd had a coffee.

"Redd, I know I get on your nerves," said Marta, "but I do like working with you, even though it's a grim job. I am honestly worried about Nathan particularly and a bit about Tom."

"Thank you. You seem quite efficient."

"Don't you like working with me, even a little bit?"

Redd smiled. "Well, I don't think you're bullshitting me. I think you're telling me the truth. Or the truth as you know it."

"What does that mean, 'the truth as I know it'? Isn't truth, truth?"

"I just mean, that you are telling me what you have been told or have understood about what your son and husband have been up to. You aren't making anything up."

"How is that the truth as I know it? You're confusing me."

"I'm sorry. Let me explain. It's not a criticism. What I'm saying is that you have lived with a con man for so long that you process what you hear from him, and now your son also, in a different way than I probably would. What appears normal to you might set off an alarm bell with me."

"I think you're saying I'm stupid again. Screw you."

"No. What I'm saying is that there may be things that he and your son have talked about that seem normal to you, but they wouldn't to me. That's all. I think you are quite clever."

"I guess I'll accept that. So, you do like working with me?"

"Lord, help me, yes."

"That's all I wanted to hear. And even though I think it would be fun to get you into bed, I appreciate the fact that you like me for my mind and not just for my body." She laughed as they stood up from the table. "Actually, now I am bullshitting you."

33

Fits and Starts

Marta placed the box with the papers from the desk on the front seat of the truck between the two of them and started to sort through. "Here's something. I missed this yesterday. It was kind of folded over in the corner, I guess. It looks like one of those thumb drive things you stick in the USB ports. It was in this envelope with a badge thing. Hmmm. BHA. British Horse Racing Authority. Guest badge for something. Yes. How the hell did I miss all this stuff? I guess it wasn't art related. Well back to the dunce category for me. There's a folder here, guest of Sir Anthony Howe."

"Was it for Nathan or for your husband?" asked Redd.

"Let me look. Doesn't say."

"Is there a date?"

"Yes, six months ago. Cheltenham something. That's not when Tom and I were there, and this Cheltenham place doesn't ring a bell. We didn't go there or near there."

"Anything else?"

"Not so far. What can we do with that name?"

"Since it's Sir whomever, we should be able to find him very easily. There is a listing of all of the peerages with background and so forth."

"The old money type that Tom always looked up to."

"Sometimes, and nowadays old former money. Having a title doesn't automatically make you rich."

"How do you know that?"

"Kathryn went to university and lived in Scotland for a number of years, and her brother worked in the UK. They have both told me a bit about life there. They both ran into people from that class from time to time."

"Ah, another thing to compete with. A European education." She laughed, and Redd ignored it.

"This could mean something. It's the first real name we have. But don't get your hopes too high. It could just be someone he met at a gallery opening or some such and it was just a one-time invitation. It doesn't necessarily mean it will lead us anywhere. But it's more than we had a few hours ago, so let's hope."

"What will you do now?" asked Marta.

"I'll look him up on the computer when I get back, but I'll also send his name to an FBI contact and see if, by chance, they have anything on him through the British police or Interpol. I don't know if they work as closely since Brexit, but they might. There is still international crime."

"Should I keep going through this stuff? I guess so."

They were just getting to the top of the Blue Ridge mountains and were passing the exit for the Skyline Drive, a road that had been used by kidnappers in one of Redd's earlier cases that still had a few loose ends.

"See if there are any references to anything in London," said Redd.

"Yeah, just because you're a duke or an earl or a whatever, doesn't mean you live in a castle or a great big manor house, I guess. You can also have a nice place in London. Have you spent much time in England?"

"Not a lot, but I was there on a case recently. I don't think we were far from Cheltenham, in fact. I recall the sign on the motorway."

"What case was that?"

"I can't really talk about it. It had to do with events a long time ago."

"Was it a sad case?"

"That's a funny thing to ask. Yes, it was. Quite sad, in fact."

"Did it involve murder?"

"In the end, yes, but I can't really discuss it."

"That's okay. Was the murder in England?" she asked, ignoring his response.

Herring smiled. "You're persistent, aren't you? No, the murder was not in England. Have you been to England a lot? Do you like the country?"

"It's okay, a lot of the food sucks. I like Paris better, and I used to like Rome, but not so much anymore."

"Why is that?"

"Too many tourists, not as many good restaurants. I don't know, it's just changed. More than Paris, I think."

"You seem to know a lot about Europe," said Redd.

"Are you surprised?"

"In a way. Not that many Americans know Europe that well."

"Before I met Tom, I had a boyfriend who was very adventurous, and we spent six months bumming around Europe on the cheap and having sex. Then I met Tom, and when he had a success with one of his ventures we'd go to Europe and spend a bunch of money and maybe have a little less sex. But still fun."

"Back to the box there," said Redd. "Anything else of interest? You said a thumb drive?"

"Yeah, in this envelope with the badge and some other papers. Maybe related to the BHA thing."

"We can get into it when we get back and see what it shows."

"That's about it. Are we going back to the big house on the hill?"

"There isn't a computer there that we can use for this. I'll drop you off at the hotel and call you if I come up with anything."

"Redd, I am about to go batty at that hotel. There is nothing to do and nowhere to go. Let me come with you. I promise to behave."

Redd thought about it for a few seconds. "Alright, let's go see what's on this drive. After that I have some personal stuff to take care of."

"How about I take you and your girlfriend out to dinner? That's allowed, isn't it? By the way, are you going to charge me some huge fee for trying to find my son and husband? I suppose I should have asked that early on."

"The FBI doesn't usually charge citizens for its services. And I'm on contract with them. So you won't get a bill from me."

"Well, that's good to know. By the way, am I ever going to get to go home? Not that I necessarily want to go back to that god-forsaken place. But when are we going to resolve something on that?"

"As soon as we either locate your family or we catch the guys who are looking for you."

"I didn't know you were looking for those guys."

"The agency has a notice out, but we don't have an active manhunt, no. We don't have anything to go on at this point. We need to work backward."

"That all sounds very open-ended," she responded. "How about I rent that big house on the hill since it's not being used right now? Then you can keep an eye on me."

"We already had this discussion."

"Well, I can't stay at that damn hotel much longer. I'll jump out a window just to relieve the boredom."

"Do you have any family you could stay with?"

"I have a sister in Oregon and a brother in the Marines. The brother is out, and the sister has three kids and not enough space for my clothes, let alone me."

Redd smiled. "Then we better get on with finding your husband and son."

They were pulling into the drive at Kathryn's house. She had not returned from school, and Douglas had gone back to Highland County.

"This is cute," said Marta. "I expected something bigger."

"She used to live here alone. Why would a person need more than this?"

They went inside, and Redd showed her into his office and started the computer.

"Can I wander around a bit?" Marta asked.

"No. Stay here, and let's see what's on this thing. You may recognize something."

The icon for the drive popped up on the screen, and Redd clicked on it. The computer whirred a bit and then asked for a password. Normally this would have stopped him and he would have had to wait for Douglas to work on accessing it, but in his notes Douglas had written that Nathan used a date-sequenced set of passwords for secondary security once you were in, but had used another static password for initial entry. Douglas had listed the string of twelve digits, numerals and special characters. Redd hoped that the password worked everywhere.

He was in luck in that the screen opened, but out of luck when it showed only lines of characters in bunches that looked like passwords or account numbers. There were no names of either institutions or of people. Presumably some part of the sequences represented a code. He would have to have Douglas look at it after all. He tried clicking on some of the lines but nothing happened.

"I don't think we're going to get anywhere with this. I'll have to have my expert work on it," he said to Marta, who was looking over his shoulder.

"How long will that take?"

"I have to go out to Highland County and get him to come over here to do it. He's offline."

"That must be brutal. Should we leave now? I'm not doing anything else."

"No, it's too late. He was just here last night."

"Is he cute? He must be, since his sister is beautiful."

"I'm sure he's good looking. I'm not a good judge of that. But he's a recluse. I don't think you'd have much luck. In fact, I know you wouldn't have any luck. And you would definitely not care for the lifestyle. He doesn't have a phone, TV, internet, or a connection to any normal utility."

"Sheesh. That's radical. How does he know all this computer technology then?"

"He designed a lot of it a few years ago and then began to believe that what he was doing was not in the best interest of the human race and dropped out."

"And now he lives in the woods. Huh. You're right. Not my thing. But he could still be cute. Mountain man type."

Redd had to laugh in spite of himself.

At that moment he heard a vehicle turning into the drive and a door slam. He was in the process of ejecting the thumb drive from the computer when he heard Kathryn call out as she came in the back door. "Hello?"

"Hi—I'm in the office with Marta. Come on back."

Marta turned as Kathryn came into the room with a small attaché case in one hand and her gloves in another. Kathryn put down the case and said, "Hi, I'm Kathryn. How's it going?"

"I'm Marta. Nice to meet you. It's fits and starts. This is a lovely house."

"Thank you. Redd, you making progress? Marta, it's your son and husband missing in Europe? I'm very sorry. Redd, did you find anything today?"

"Hi, possibly. I need Douglas again, but we may have found something. I was just about to take Marta back to the hotel. She found a thumb drive, but it appears to be coded."

"Oh, too bad you didn't have it last night. But he'll be back maybe tomorrow. He had to order a part for his truck. Something he really needs for it. I saw him before he left. Marta, you want to stay for dinner? Unless you're a vegetarian. I got a couple of lamb racks. It's enough for three. I have plenty of veggies."

"Are you sure? I don't want to impose."

"You're not. You okay with that Redd? I'll take her over to the farm to see the cows, and then we'll fix up something."

"Fine with me," said Redd. "I need to send a request to Berry right now, if you don't need me."

"I just need to change. I'll loan Marta a jacket, so she doesn't get dirty at the barn. We're about the same size. By the way, she's not a suspect, is she? I don't want to interfere in the case."

"No, as far as I can tell she's not. Marta?" said Redd.

"God help me, of course not. I didn't do anything to either one. I'm trying to get them back."

"He has to ask," said Kathryn. "I was a suspect in one case."

"You?" said Marta. "Surely not."

"Can you both drop this?" admonished Redd. Kathryn had turned to go out the door. Marta gave him a look, and he would have sworn that if they had been in elementary school she would have stuck her tongue out at him.

34

Maternal Instinct

Kathryn's comment about her being a suspect at one point set off a chain of thoughts in Redd's mind. It was true that when Kathryn's father and stepmom had been found shot to death, Kathryn did not have a solid alibi for the time of their deaths. But she had no motive for the crime, and the complexity of events surrounding it had ruled her out as he investigated.

Those thoughts brought him around to Gabe's situation in Charlottesville. None of it made sense from the get-go, assuming Gabe was telling the truth. He was inclined to believe that Gabe was being set up, but by whom? If he was going to take on this case, he would need to look at the family finances, interview Gabe's wife, and do a background check on both of them as well as look into the life and finances of the missing woman, Sandy. He realized that a man's freedom was in jeopardy, but it all smacked of a domestic dispute, a sordid affair or tryst that had gone wrong, and he had no appetite for looking into those kinds of things when so much worse was happening all around him.

He stopped himself for a moment. Was he being callous? There was a missing woman, and blood had been found. But the sequence of events made no sense, and in situations like this it was Redd's experience that a key piece was missing and the case was not at all what it seemed. He decided to sleep on it for the night and would talk to Gabe's attorney in the morning. He thought there might be a way to oversee an investigation if the attorneys could do some groundwork for him. He had recently had to dig into minutiae while looking for a killer or killers, and it could be mind-numbing.

He made an outline of tasks for the following day, and by the time he had finished, Kathryn and Marta were coming back into the house. Kathryn was explaining her philosophy about raising calves, which he was surprised to find might be of interest to Marta. He was not surprised to hear Marta respond to a comment about breeding. "So, the cows don't even get to have real sex? How sad."

Kathryn laughed. "I don't think it is quite as important to the cows as it is to us."

Marta smiled at Redd when she spotted him coming into the kitchen. "I'm learning how to raise cattle. Maybe that's a business my husband could get into when he gets back from Europe. This is pretty fancy."

"I kind of doubt it," he said. "It requires some special training. I don't see you as a farmer's wife, either."

She laughed. "No, probably not. Where can I wash my hands around here?"

Redd pointed down the hall to the bathroom.

Kathryn had pulled off her boots and stepped into the room. "So how was your new protégé?" Redd asked with a smile.

"Jeez," she replied. "What a live wire. She was actually genuinely interested, almost like a kid. I think she's probably quite smart, but just a bit unfocused." She said the last two sentences in a low voice so that Marta wouldn't hear. "I actually like her. But I think I better keep a closer eye on you. She's pretty hot.

Before she comes back, have you made any progress? Are you any closer to finding her son and husband?"

"No, they just seem to have vanished without a trace. Until we can figure out what they were really up to, I don't even know where to start."

Marta came back into the room, and Kathryn invited her to take a seat. "Would you like a glass of wine, something stronger?" she asked.

"That would be divine," Marta replied. "Wine is great. Is there anything I can do to help?"

"No, I was just asking Redd about the case. It must be very difficult for both of them to be missing?"

"I'm most worried about my son. I've actually been worried for some time about my husband's influence on Nathan. We spoiled him, I'm afraid, and my husband has always been into some kind of con."

"Why did you put up with that?" asked Kathryn. "If you don't mind my asking. I don't mean to be rude, but you seem pretty sharp and sophisticated."

"I'm not offended. I've asked myself the same thing a few times. And Redd asked me. I guess it was just easy. I grew up poor, and my first husband was handsome but not very ambitious, as it turned out."

"He's the father of your son, right—not Tom, who is missing?"

"Right. I got divorced when Nathan was about five, and he and Tom hit it off, and he wanted me to change his last name to McFerren. I have to say, for a person who's not very honest, he's been a very good father. Oops, I guess I should say a good father as far as caring about his inherited son, but maybe not so good as a role model."

"Did your son go to college?"

"He started in business, but he got bored and dropped out. He talked his way into a job in a bank for a while, but he was lots more interested in what his stepdad was up to. He was sort of looking for a way to get rich quick."

"Are you two close?" asked Kathryn. "I never had kids, obviously, and won't. So I don't have a feeling for the maternal instinct. Or maybe I transferred it to my cows," Katherine laughed.

"Yes and no. I can't say I ever had a great maternal instinct either. If I hadn't gotten pregnant with my first husband, I wouldn't have had kids either. In one respect, Nathan is lucky that his stepdad took as much interest in him as he did. I would probably have let him become a juvenile delinquent. I was too lenient. I just hope he didn't become something worse as a result."

Kathryn had put a bottle of Chardonnay on the table and told Marta to serve herself. Kathryn had a glass, and Redd poured himself a half glass as he helped with dinner. "Oh dear," said Marta after a few minutes. "I'm afraid I wasn't paying attention and drank all the rest of this wine. Where are my manners?"

"No worries," said Kathryn. "We're going to have a red with the lamb. You've had a tough day and a tough week."

She went to the wine cabinet under the counter and pulled out one of the lower racks and selected a bottle labelled The Prisoner, a heavy California blend that would go well with the stronger taste of the lamb. The meat had roasted in the oven for twenty-five minutes, and there was a rice pilaf, some steamed broccoli, and a Boston lettuce salad with artichoke hearts, pine nuts, and a few croutons. Redd opened the wine so that it could breathe for a few minutes and set the table.

During dinner the conversation switched to cities they had visited in Europe, in spite of the presumption that somewhere in one of those cities, Marta's son and husband had gone missing. Marta ate heartily and congratulated Kathryn on the dinner and offered to clean up, but Kathryn refused her help. Redd poured Marta a small glass of Port and invited her to take a seat in a wing chair near the unlit fireplace. He and Kathryn did not normally have an after-dinner drink, but Marta was still fidgety in spite of the Chardonnay and the dinner wine. Redd thought the Port might help.

She accepted the small glass and took a large sip and set it on the table beside the chair.

A moment later she finished the port and put the glass back on the table, and in another minute was fast asleep in the comfortable chair.

Kathryn looked at Redd. "If you can get her on her feet, put her in the guest room. You'll never get her back to the hotel in this state. And you shouldn't drive anyway."

A few minutes later they had her settled under a blanket in the guest room bed.

Once they were cozy in their own bedroom, Kathryn laughed quietly and said to Redd, "Fascinating. I don't really know what to make of her or how judgmental to be. Let's just hope we don't wake up with her in bed between us."

35

How Do I Look?

When he woke up in the morning, Redd's mind was made up. He would look into the case of the missing woman and her potential murder. He had dreamed about a version of events over and over, with women coming and going from the dreams in various stages of dress or undress.

He got up with Kathryn and went out to do chores, leaving Marta asleep in the guest room. When they came back by 8:00, she was up and sitting at the kitchen table looking at her phone.

"I hope you don't mind, but I borrowed a charger for a few minutes and took a shower."

"Of course not," said Kathryn. "Would you like some breakfast?"

"Oh Lord no, just coffee, or I can get some at the hotel. If you can call me a taxi, if such a thing exists around here."

"No, don't worry," said Redd. "Coffee will be ready in a few minutes, and I'll drop you at the hotel on my way to Charlottesville. I need to go back for another matter."

She nodded and went back to looking at her phone. She looked surprisingly fresh for not having had a chance to put on makeup or do whatever she would normally have done in the mornings to her appearance. Perhaps she didn't need a lot of help. Her clothes were slightly wrinkled, but did not look slept in. She must have awakened and taken them off during the night.

After he had showered and shaved, Redd had a coffee and a cinnamon muffin, and he and Marta left for Staunton. Douglas was due back at some time that day to pick up an auto part. Redd was eager to hand him the drive they found the day before in the envelope at the bottom of the file box.

As soon as they pulled out of the driveway in Redd's pickup, Marta spoke up. "Redd, thank you for last night and for putting up with me, but can I please just ride along to Charlottesville with you? I just need to stop by the hotel to change clothes, and I won't hold you up but a minute. I promise. Then you can just drop me at Barracks Road, and I'll go shopping."

"You are persistent," said Redd. "I guess so. But I don't know how long I'll be." He had texted a note to the attorney that he would be over early, and he'd gotten a positive response.

Marta was surprisingly true to her word and took only five minutes to change into another pair of tight jeans, a different cashmere sweater and scarf, but the same boots and jacket as the day before. She had put on lipstick and brushed her hair and looked remarkable for so little effort. She unzipped the jacket as she got in and smiled at Redd. "How do I look?"

Redd laughed. "You look good." And he shook his head.

They talked about the farm for the first part of the trip, with Marta asking about the background. Then she asked Redd about his life and his career as a sheriff. She didn't ask about his wife, Mary, but Redd could tell that Kathryn must have mentioned her. At one point Marta said something about the stability of his life, not all of which Redd caught. Then she turned pensive and quiet until they reached Barracks Road Shopping Center which was close to the law offices. Redd agreed to text her when he was through with his meetings.

36

Self-Serving Nonsense

When Redd arrived at the lawyer's office, Gabe and his attorney were already there. Redd was shown to the conference room where they were meeting.

After customary greetings, Redd took a seat. "I'm willing to look into this for you, but I won't have the time to do all of the detail work that might be needed. As long as Lawrence here can provide research assistance and a person from time to time to possibly look into connections and family histories, I'll do all I can. I want to warn you that I am involved in another matter right now, and depending on what I find, I'll have to give that priority. Is that suitable for you?"

"That works, but I'm not sure why you would need to go into family background," said Gabe. "We don't have that much history, and it's from a decade or more ago."

"I need to go into it, because whatever has really taken place here is most likely driven by something in the past. If you aren't willing to cooperate, then I won't work with you," replied Redd sternly.

"No, no, I didn't mean that…"

Lawrence interrupted. "We'll work with you however you wish. And I have a young investigator who is thorough and diligent and whose services I'll provide. You can meet her after we sort out the details of what you want."

"Alright, that works for me," said Redd. "I'd like to get some basics down right now. First, I need someone to find the flight records and rental car information for the missing woman. And see if she had a flight reserved for the return trip and what the date was. And anything else we can come up with. Next of kin, ex-husband. You said she was divorced, right?"

"Yes, not so long ago."

"You told me her parents and sister are dead. Did she have any children?"

"No, not that I know of."

"Did you know the sister that took her own life?"

Gabe paused. "Ah, not really. I had limited interactions with her in college."

"Oh, so you did know her?"

"No. I just said, I knew *of* her—met her once or twice, but nothing more."

Redd had a feeling that there was more to it than Gabe let on, but he let it go for the moment. "Why did she kill herself, do you know?"

"I heard it was drug related. I think she got in with the wrong crowd and got hooked on drugs."

"You didn't talk about it the night you spent with Sandy, her sister?"

"No, it didn't come up."

"So, tell me," said Redd. "I don't care what you do or don't do, but how did you arrange this visit with Sandy, especially after so much time? Had you been in regular contact with her over the years? Give me some background on this."

"Like I mentioned, I knew her in college, when I was in law

school and she was undergrad. She was in the same sorority as my wife, and I saw her at various parties and so on. But we never went out. She had a couple of boyfriends and was a bit wild, but I never did anything with her."

"Was she a friend of your wife's?"

"Not close, more like an acquaintance. You know how sorority sisters are."

"No, but okay. Back to this visit a couple of days ago. How did that come about?"

"Uh, I got an email from her that she was going to be in the area to do some research on family stuff. I think I told you that she had been working for a tech company, and our firm had done some legal work for them, and we had been in touch professionally over the years, but not so much in the last year or so. The firm wasn't developing anything new, and then she got divorced and was moving to Sacramento."

"Did she want to come and see both you and your wife? Did your wife know she was coming?"

Gabe hesitated. "I didn't tell Celia about it. If I can be perfectly honest...?"

"That would be a good idea," said Redd.

"I had always kind of had the hots for Sandy, and I thought this might be an opportunity to, you know..."

"Is this something you do regularly, set up meetings with women for sex?"

Gabe jumped up from the table. "Listen, damn it, that has nothing to do with this."

"Oh, sit down," said Redd. "It might have everything to do with it. Maybe your wife found out about affairs and decided to punish you for it. Maybe she and Sandy were in it together and are trying to scare you."

"That's preposterous. Sandy wouldn't have had sex with me if that was the case. Are you serious?"

"Just testing a hypothesis. So, did you or didn't you have affairs from time to time?"

"Christ, yes, but nothing serious, just the occasional fling. My wife isn't as interested in sex as she used to be, and I don't think she really cares that much."

"What's her response been to this?" asked Redd.

Gabe looked at Lawrence and was silent for a few moments before answering. "Uh, she's not happy. She's locked me out, and I'm staying at a hotel."

Redd just looked at Gabe without commenting. He had thought all along that Gabe's answers were self-serving nonsense and that he was excusing his philandering by blaming a supposedly frigid wife. That was a classic trope for so many men. He had encountered it in domestic cases as sheriff, and it ran across all classes of society.

"I'll need to talk to your wife, and I need the names of as many of your old classmates as you can give me. Can you get me some contact info for them? And I need the address and contact info for Sandy and her ex-husband, if you have that."

"I don't understand what you need all that for," protested Gabe again. "I need you to find Sandy and see why she disappeared like that, or find whoever really kidnapped or took her. Find out what really happened. I did not—I tell you—I did not hurt that woman. And I sure as hell didn't kill her. I wanted to hook up with her again, if you must know. Why would I kill her?"

"Well, if someone else did take her, then talking to everyone in her life, like her old friends, ex, former colleagues, maybe that will turn up a reason or a clue. You're an attorney. Surely you've done background research for cases before. Or I certainly hope so."

Gabe looked suddenly deflated. "Yes, of course. I'll get you a list as soon as this meeting is over. But what are you going to do in the meantime?"

"I'm going to go talk to your wife right now, and I'll stop by later and pick up the list, or better yet, email it to me. Here's a card with the address and my phone number. I'll then parcel out what I need to work on and what Lawrence's researcher can do."

Redd stood up, and Lawrence told Gabe to wait while he showed Redd out. When they had left the conference room, he closed the door and motioned for Redd to come with him to his office. He closed the door and turned to Redd.

"You don't seem to like my client. Where are you going with this? Do you think he really killed that woman?"

"I'm actually quite ambivalent about your client. No, I don't think he killed that woman, Sandy. But I think he *is* lying about some of the background with her. Or maybe about something in the business relationship? I don't know. The pieces in this don't make sense, and I was just trying to shake something loose."

"Okay. I guess I get your meaning. What do you want us to do?"

"For the moment, can you check out the history of the work he did for her firm, at least to the extent that you can, and get me financials for him and his wife, a personal balance sheet or something like that. Just to see if there are any financial issues that might be hidden. I assume he isn't in trouble with any loan sharks or such and that he isn't being punished for a debt or something equally strange. Did the police take his phone and computer?"

"Yeah, but they should be through with them by now. What do you want from them?"

"Just check his phone record and see if there are any calls he can't explain. Also, unless he blocked it, which most people don't, you can see where he went minute by minute, as you know, from the tracking that's built in. It's worth looking at further, the police already did part of it. And then his list of former classmates and any family info."

"Got it. I'll let you know when I have something for you."

"Once I get all that, I'll let you know if I need your researcher to do a few things."

"Okay, and I'll text you his wife's cell number so you can let her know you're on the way."

Herring texted Marta when he got to his truck and told her he had one more meeting to take care of, and then he could pick her up. She responded that she was in a coffee shop and was in no rush.

37

No Money Problems

Redd's phone pinged with a new text message, the number for Celia, Gabe's wife. He decided to text her before attempting to call, so that she would be more likely to answer. A few moments later he had a positive response, and he called her.

"Good morning, Mrs. Dunbar, this is Reddford Herring. I've been hired by your husband and his law firm to investigate and try to get to the bottom of this case. I wondered if I could meet with you this morning?"

"And just who are you anyway? I'm not sure I want to meet with anybody right now."

"I used to be the sheriff over in Augusta County."

"Oh right, the kidnapping case, I remember something about that now. So, what are you doing for my husband again?"

"He has asked me to try to find the woman who was at your house and to prove his innocence in the matter. It would really help if I could talk to you."

"I'm so angry with him right now, I'm not sure I'd give you a straight answer."

"I think I understand. But do you really think your husband is capable of murder?"

She was quiet for a few moments. "Really and truly, no, but something went on here."

"So it seems. I would really appreciate just a few minutes of your time right now, if you can do that. Your impressions and background will be very valuable."

"I suppose so. But wait, you said you used to be sheriff. So, what are you now? A private detective?"

"No, I'm on call for the FBI for special cases, but I'm doing this for the law firm as a private matter. I recommended that your husband use a detective firm, but I've done some work with his law firm in the past, and together they wanted me to work on this for them. I agreed as a favor."

"Alright. Well, I'm home right now. Do you have the address?"

"Yes. I'll be there in a few minutes."

When Redd pulled into the driveway, he noticed that all of the curtains and blinds were closed, and the house looked as if no one was there. But when he sounded the doorbell, it was answered quickly by an attractive brunette dressed in tight black exercise clothes, which clearly showed off all of the curves and crevasses of her body. Redd noted that it felt even more revealing and sexy than if she had been nude. Gabe had said she wasn't all that interested in sex, and Kathryn had told Redd that just because a woman dressed in a sexy manner didn't really mean they were interested. Sometimes they just wanted to look good or look hot. It confused him. He realized this was the kind of thinking that got men in trouble.

"Do you have some sort of ID?" she asked, as he stepped into the hallway and she closed the door behind him. It would have been a bit late to have stopped him if he weren't who he said he was.

He showed her an embossed FBI identification card that Wendell had issued for him. She glanced at it and looked at

Redd and nodded. "Let's go sit in the breakfast room, if that's okay. I was just about to do some yoga, but that can wait. What do you want to know?"

Redd followed her to a room off of the kitchen where there was a table and several comfortable chairs. She had opened the plantation shutter blades to let in a little light.

"Would you like some coffee, or iced tea?"

"No thanks. I appreciate you taking the time to talk to me. I'll try to make this quick."

She shrugged. Celia was quite fit. Her face, which was just a bit too long and severe to be called heart shaped, could still be very pretty if she smiled. But it was a bit off-putting with the creased frown she now displayed.

"I'm not sure where to start," said Redd. "I take it you didn't know your old friend Sandy would be visiting?"

"Hell no, and she wasn't really that close a friend, and I hadn't seen her for years anyway."

"But you knew your husband stayed in touch with her. I mean for business?"

"Yes, but not for a while, I don't think. I mean he used to mention it from time to time, but not lately. And I sure as hell didn't know she was going to be here a few days ago."

"Where were you?"

"I was in Atlanta. I had a family meeting that was set up a few months ago, about some family money and some property that needed to be sold. But my uncle got sick, and we had to postpone. So, I came home early."

"And your husband didn't plan to go?"

"It isn't his family. No need."

"Does him having this night with Sandy surprise you? I'm sorry, but I have to ask."

"With her, yes and no. I thought he had the hots for her a long time ago but didn't think he still did."

"Again, I'm sorry to have to ask, but do you think he fooled around otherwise?"

"I don't know. I never caught him at it, but I wondered a few times. Did he?"

"You'll have to ask him."

"That's probably an answer in itself. With this happening it seems highly likely. He's very attractive to women."

"He mentioned that Sandy had a sister who had taken her own life. What do you know about that?"

"Not much. Nothing really. She got into drugs is what I heard. I didn't keep up with either of them, as I think I already said. I don't know why you're going there."

"Just background. Now, back to you two. Finances. Do you have any financial issues—any problems with loans, credit cards, anything like that? Gabe doesn't gamble or have gambling debts?"

"God, no. He's never been into anything like that. He isn't even in a local football pool, as much as he likes sports. And we have no money problems. I have money from my family. I don't even see how that is relevant. You just seem to be fishing. What are you really trying to get at? This is beginning to piss me off."

"I'm sorry. I'm just trying to eliminate as many of the things that lead to murder."

"Murder, what the fuck? Do you really think Gabe killed Sandy? That's crazy. I think I want you to leave." And she stood up.

Redd remained seated. "Mrs. Dunbar, you do realize I've been hired to prove your husband *didn't* kill Sandy, right?"

She had started to walk away but turned back, her face red. "Well, this is a very strange way to go about it. I still want you to leave now. I'll let you know if I want to talk to you again. Now go, please."

Redd stood up. "Fine, but it's better me asking these questions than the police, and people who have the opposite objective for your husband. You let me know when we can continue our discussions."

She hesitated and seemed about to relent, but by then Redd was at the door. He opened it and stepped out. Clearly, she had something to hide, and it would be good to let her think for a while about the consequences of sending him away.

When he got back to the coffee shop, he went in and picked up a latte and Marta. For once he was glad to see her.

38

Holy Shit!

"So, how's your morning been?"

"It was of some value. Lots of questions asked and a few questions answered," Redd responded.

"I don't suppose you are going to tell me what it is all about, are you?"

"I told you I couldn't the other day."

"Okay. How about I tell you?"

"What?"

"Well," she said, "I looked it up on my phone. And I found that a certain lawyer is suspected of killing his girlfriend after an orgy at a big house here in Charlottesville, and he buried her body, and they can't find it and the police raided the house. Am I close? What else would attract the attention of a big-time sheriff like yourself."

"Ex. Ex-sheriff. Wait a minute. There's nothing like that in the newspaper."

"No, of course not, but somebody started a blog thing, and its full of comments."

"Almost none of that is accurate."

"Aha, but there is something," she laughed. "And here you come to save the day."

"Jesus, the internet," he replied. "I will admit to looking at the facts of the case, but that's it. Social media is so full of crap. Is there anything about your husband and son out there?"

Marta looked over at him, suddenly surprised at the question. "I hadn't thought about that. Not that I know of. There wasn't ever a news story, so no one really knows about it. Just you and me and your girlfriend."

"The local cops knew something was going on when you called them about the break-in. There would have been something in the weekly paper about it."

"But there's no local connection to them being missing," she replied. "They went missing over in Europe. That's where the issue is."

"No, that's where you're wrong. The issue, their disappearance, is as much connected with here as it is with Europe. This gives me an idea about something I should have thought about before. We need to turn around and head back into Charlottesville."

"Where are we going?"

"To the airport."

"Oh good. Are we going somewhere?"

"No, but I want to see if I can borrow a dog."

"Everything is a freaking riddle with you. How do you ever talk a woman into going to bed with you? She'd have lost interest and found someone else and married them by the time you got to first base."

Redd laughed. "I'm going to see if TSA has a drug sniffing dog they can bring out to your son's shop."

"Hold on—my son and husband aren't into drugs. That is way too big-time and dangerous. And they don't like drugs."

"Uh-uh, so are arson and money laundering and financial fraud, but your husband had a finger in all those pies. I should have thought about drugs when we were out there. I was just focused on artwork, but the more I've been thinking about it, the less likely that seems. There just isn't enough money in it. So, it has to be something else. Drugs, a natural conclusion."

"This is really disturbing, Sheriff. I don't like it at all."

"Neither do I, but don't you want to find your son and husband?"

"Of course, but this is really scary to think about." She was quiet for a few moments, and then Redd realized she was starting to cry and her shoulders were heaving. "Oh god, I just don't want to believe this. Drug people are so vicious; I just don't want to believe it. They could be dead. Oh, what am I going to do? I just can't think about this."

Redd pulled up to the curb just past the airport terminal and put a police business sign in the window. He was glad to see a police car parked nearby. An officer got out and came toward him. Redd spoke quickly to him and the officer nodded and came to stand near the truck as Redd requested.

Redd tapped on Marta's window, and she rolled it down. "Just stay here, and I'll be back in a minute. The officer here is going to keep an eye on the truck. I'll be right back."

Just over five minutes later Redd was back, looked around, thanked the officer, and got in.

"Tomorrow morning, TSA is going to get a drug-sniffing dog down here from Dulles airport, and they will meet us at the art frame shop, and we'll have the dog sniff around to see if cocaine or something else has ever been there."

"So, what are you thinking, Redd? What does the artwork have to do with drugs?"

"I'm wondering if maybe your son has been making frames that could be filled with drugs and welded shut. Maybe that's the real business."

"Holy shit," she said. "I sure as hell hope not. If they are doing that, I'm divorcing that son of a bitch. And disowning my son. Jesus."

Redd didn't say anything, but if his theory was correct, then there might no longer be a husband to divorce or a son to disown. He was also thinking that he might have been a bit cavalier in his thoughts about Marta's safety.

He realized there could be forces at work that might be a danger. There was a momentary sense that he and Marta had possibly been followed in Charlottesville. It might have been his imagination, a slowly developing picture, assembled from pieces over the past few days. The men shooting out the doors and barging into the house. The sheer violence of it contributed to a suspicion that drugs and all that drugs entail could be involved. He rolled these thoughts over in his mind on the drive back to Staunton.

Of course, drugs had always been a possibility, but what he had seen of the apartment and the frame shop seemed convincing, to speak to a real focus on bogus art. Or perhaps some kind of money laundering through artificial pricing for artwork. Marta was right. Drug smugglers were vicious, and nothing in Tom's past showed any tendency toward such an activity. But life means nothing in the drug business, and once you were in you were trapped. Redd hoped the dog wouldn't find any residue the next morning.

As a courtesy, he called the Charlottesville police department and told them that he would be at the framing shop in the morning with someone from TSA and a dog. He asked them to keep an eye on the place and invited them to stop in to see if anything was found.

Marta was more subdued on the drive back. Redd wondered if she had just been fooling herself all along, lying to herself about the reality of two people going missing, refusing to admit that cheating people as a way of making a living was also an excellent way to make enemies of them. At some point, that caught up with a person. And depending on the person being cheated, the payback could be fatal.

39

More Than Luck

The silence of the drive also allowed him to think a bit more clearly about Marta herself and the danger she might be in. If drugs were involved and there was an international component to it, then she was a probable target. Whoever had come to the house and shot it up was clearly looking for something or for some person.

By the time they got to Staunton, he had made a decision.

"Marta, I don't want you to stay here at the hotel tonight, but I don't want you to check out either," he said as they pulled up.

"What? What do you want me to do? I'd be more than happy to get out of that place. Are you shipping me off somewhere, so I won't keep pestering you?"

"No, but I don't think the men who came to your house are done looking for you, or whatever it is that's missing."

"Why do you suddenly think this?" she asked. "You haven't seemed all that concerned up to now."

Redd thought for a minute as they sat in the driveway with the truck idling. "I was assuming the men were looking for your husband and son, and when they didn't find them, they would give up and go away. But now, I'm not so sure. The fact that they hadn't been to your son's apartment or the shop tells me they were, or are, working with limited information. I don't know what that means. Except that they aren't local, maybe not even from the US, and maybe are getting directions from someone somewhere else who had to measure the implications. Since you haven't heard anything new from Tom or Nathan, we obviously have no clue what's going on."

"You think they are dead, don't you?"

"I have no idea," Redd lied to her. "There is no way to tell at this point. I hope not. But I do think we should keep you better protected."

She smiled in spite of herself at that. "What do you propose? Sending me off to the woods with the recluse?"

Redd laughed. "He'd lock you in the woodshed. No, I want you to go up and get enough clothes for overnight and something to cover your head with. Do you have a hoody or a hooded jacket of some kind?"

"You want to sneak me out of here?"

"Sort of."

"This is scaring me. Are we being followed?"

"I don't think so, but I don't feel right. There's too much we don't know. So, I'm going to pull out and go around the corner. Do you know the town layout? Have you walked around any?"

"A little. It isn't exactly Manhattan—you can see the whole place in ten minutes."

"You know where the college is, Mary Baldwin?"

"Yeah, up on the hill, two blocks away."

"Okay, you have a backpack, right?"

"Yes, you saw it."

"Okay, just put a few things in it, don't bring anything else except that and your purse. And go out on the far side of the lobby. When you come out of the elevators, to your left is a door to the garage. Go into the garage and out through the entrance on the far side of the hotel. Keep your head covered. You can put a scarf around your neck and cover your mouth a bit but don't be too obvious."

"I got it, I got it. Where do I meet you?"

"Turn right toward the college and go up to the end of the street and turn right and go two blocks. A winding street comes down the hill there. I'll meet you there in ten or fifteen minutes. When you see the truck, get in the back seat and lay flat."

"Redd, I don't like this. You're scaring me. You saw someone, the guys at the house..."

"No, I didn't see anyone, but I'm worried they will figure out where you are, maybe, and we've been lucky so far. I want to keep that luck going. More than luck. Care."

"Okay, okay. Can't you wait for me in the garage?"

"No, that's no good. Just go. I tell you what. I'll let you out and I'll go up and park the truck and walk back down the way I told you to come. Don't speak to me or anything. I'll just be there to watch over you. Now go."

Marta reached across the seat and squeezed his hand. She smiled tightly and got out of the truck.

Ten minutes later, Redd was standing at the top of the hill in front of Mary Baldwin as a woman in hiking shoes with a backpack and a hooded sweatshirt with a fancy logo on one side made her way across the street and up the hill. She walked with the determined pace of a much younger person and slowed slightly when she saw Redd at the intersection of the two streets. He walked on, and she followed, and a few minutes later they were headed to the farm with Marta steadying herself and trying not to fall off the small back seat of the cab-and-a-half truck.

40

Russian, Maybe?

When they were finally out of town and on a less winding and hilly road, Redd told Marta she could sit up.

"Jesus, I feel like a tossed salad," she said, sitting up and pulling her hoody down and fluffing her hair into place. "What are you going to do with me? You're not planning to put me up in that house on the hill by myself, are you?"

"No. I need to talk to Kathryn. And I'm going to update my contact at the bureau and see if he's had any developments. I think he would have let me know, but I'm going to fill him in on where you are and what we found at the little shop. I don't think I gave him a complete update last time we talked."

"I know this is a dumb question, but how long do you think this is going to go on? I mean, it will soon be a month since my son left and then my husband a bit ago and then those goons at the house. You're the sheriff, the expert. What does all this mean?"

Herring was quiet for a few moments as they turned onto the road that would lead to the farm and the turn into Kathryn's house. "I wish I knew, and I wish I could give you some assurances, but I don't know enough to even speculate. The best I can guess is that something happened when your son got to Europe that was not part of whatever arrangement he had planned, and your husband went there to fix it, and he either didn't find your son, or he did and they are together. But honestly, that's a meaningless answer. I don't know why there has been a time lag between their going to Europe and the bad guys coming to your house. If whoever they met in Europe was unhappy, I would have thought the response would have been quicker."

Marta remained silent. Herring continued. "So your husband had no communications from Nathan, your son, after he left?"

"If he did, he didn't tell me. That was supposedly why he went to find him."

"Let me ask you this, how were things between the two of you? I mean, this isn't some planned disappearance, is it? Did he owe money to the wrong people and decide to split and leave you holding the bag, hoping they wouldn't take it out on you? Is that possible?"

"God, I hope not. I don't know enough about his deals to know if he's in trouble or not. So far, he's never tangled with anyone more crooked than he is. He likes himself too much to put himself in a lot of danger."

"Sometimes you don't know how dangerous a situation can become. The guys who came to your house were not loan officers looking to warn you to pay your mortgage on time."

"Yeah, I know, I know. I don't know. I've honestly been trying to think about his recent contacts, and the one that rings the loudest bell is the guy from England. Funny, when I think about it, he had a funny accent, not really homegrown English—hard edges, like one of the eastern European languages."

"Russian, maybe? There apparently are a lot of Russians in England, London especially. I guess they and the Saudi own a lot of real estate there."

"Possibly, good manners and all that, owns some horses. But I guess everyone owns a horse in England. Did you know they have television channels that are nothing but horse races and shows and commentary and on and on? Horses, jeez."

"I saw that when I was there recently, yes."

"And Nathan did go to London first, so that connects in some little way," she said.

They were pulling into the driveway at Kathryn's house. Her work pickup was not there, so Redd backed out and headed over to the main barn which they had passed on the way in. He hadn't seen her pickup there, but she could be in one of the outer fields or at another shed.

He found her truck parked behind the large barn where she was unloading bags of protein mix for a calf self-feeder that was being set up. She didn't seem surprised to see Marta with him.

"How was your day? What's up?" she asked, looking back and forth between them.

"I'm not sure anything is up, but I'm not comfortable with what I'm learning. I had her leave most of her stuff at the hotel and sort of sneak out. I need to talk to you about some options, but let us help you with the chores, and then we can talk."

"No problem. Marta, you can help me. Redd, can you get the tractor and go move the last of the bales at the north barn? When they finish that bunch, we'll move them over to the next field. It's been too muddy down there, and I don't want them to cut it up."

Kathryn handed Marta some gloves, and Marta gamely began to move the bags as Kathryn directed. They didn't talk about anything except what they were doing, and when they were finished, Marta went along with Kathryn as she checked the heifers and some calves with runny noses, and Kathryn kept up a running commentary on the chores and why they were necessary.

Less than an hour later, the chores were finished, Redd was back with the tractor, and they headed to Kathryn's house.

As they were taking off their jackets and work shoes, Kathryn said to them both, "I'm hungry. I didn't have time for lunch today. Let's fix some dinner and have a glass of wine and then discuss what's going on."

"I'm sorry for intruding," said Marta. "I don't…"

"Don't worry about it right now. Redd will sort it out. It's what he does. You can wash up down the hall and then open some wine for us. I'll start on dinner."

41

CCTV

Redd left the two women to sort out dinner and went down the hall to his office and sent a note to Berry telling him about taking Marta out of the hotel and the arrangements to have a dog sniff for drugs at the shop tomorrow. He also asked if Berry could arrange for a safe house location for Marta temporarily and asked for any updates on the two men.

After that he called Roddy and brought him up to date on the case and asked him to have his deputies keep an eye out in his part of the county. Roddy also offered to call the local police in Staunton and ask them to keep an eye on the hotel.

Dinner was warmed-up lasagna from several days earlier and a large salad. Marta was subdued and clearly more worried than she had been on previous days. Kathryn talked about her current work, and Redd was quiet. As they were finishing dinner, Redd finally spoke up. "Kathryn, if it's okay with you, I think we should let Marta sleep in the guest room tonight. It's safe here. I sent a note to Wendell. Marta, he's the FBI guy I work with, to ask about a safe house temporarily. I just sent it, so I haven't heard back."

"That's fine with me," said Kathryn. "Marta, I don't know if Redd mentioned it, but we have good security everywhere on the farm and around the house. It's not that it's that dangerous around here generally, but the cattle are valuable, and with Redd having been sheriff, it attracts more of the wrong attention some time."

"I really don't want to inconvenience you," said Marta. "I know I've been joking around, but this is really hitting home right now."

"No problem," said Kathryn. "That all fine with you, Redd?"

"Sure," said Redd. "I also just thought of something this evening that I want to run by Wendell. Our discussions about England triggered the thought. The Brits have CCTV everywhere, and if you can give me the exact dates again of when your husband and son were in England, London specifically, then I can maybe get Wendell to have Scotland Yard or the London police send us copies of recordings for those days and locations. I should have thought of it before."

"They really do that over there?" asked Marta.

"They really do that. It's not as complete as crime shows on TV would have you believe, but it's pretty complete. And there's a lot of private coverage."

"When can we get it?"

"I don't know that we can—I just thought about it a bit ago. I'll send a note to Berry as soon as dinner is over."

This seemed to improve Marta's mood, and she hopped up and offered to clean up after dinner. Kathryn joined her, and Redd headed back to the office to call Berry, who as usual didn't answer. He left a message about the safe house again, and about requesting CCTV for London. He had looked up the retention times for coverage, and it seemed to stretch for at least 30 days. Maybe this would shed some light on who one or both of them met.

42

Under Control Now

Redd was awakened at 4:00 a.m. by the buzzing of his phone by the bed. He would normally have left it in the office, but since the office was also the spare bedroom, he had kept it with him.

The caller showed as Charlottesville police.

"Hello, this is Herring," he said.

"Mr. Herring, this is Sergeant Thomas from Charlottesville Police."

"Yes, go ahead."

"You asked us to keep an eye on a location South US 29," and he read off the address.

"Yes. What's going on?"

"There was a fire detected there about thirty minutes ago. Fire department responded, as did we—significant damage, but under control now."

"Crap. Is the structure destroyed?"

"The front section is heavily damaged. Due to the construction materials the walls are standing. The back room was less heavily damaged."

"I assume the fire was set?"

Thomas paused. "I don't want to speculate, sir, without evidence, but the firemen seemed to believe there had been an accelerant placed near the door. So yes, probably the fire was set."

"Will you keep someone on-site until we can investigate further? I was having a drug sniffing dog brought in today."

"We can do that. What time will you be here?"

"I don't know yet. I expect midmorning."

"Let us know. We will expect you."

Redd clicked off and explained to Kathryn what had happened.

"It appears you were right to be concerned," she said to Redd.

"Yeah, it wasn't anything specific, but I wondered if we were being tailed. I never spotted anyone, but it seemed inevitable unless they already knew about the place. And I think they would have broken in already if they had. I don't get it. I can't figure out who these people are."

"Do you need to leave now?"

"No, there's nothing to do until the drug dog gets there. I don't know if they can smell anything after a fire or not."

Redd turned off the bedside light and was pulling the covers back up when his phone rang again. It was the Staunton Police department.

"This is Herring."

"Mr. Herring, this is officer Lewis of the Staunton Police department. I was given your number by the desk Sergeant. Sorry to call at this hour."

"No problem. What's the issue?"

"There was a disturbance at the hotel where you had asked us to keep an eye on, or the county offices did anyway."

"Yes, that's right. What was the nature of the incident?"

"Someone tried to get into one of the guest rooms on the sixth floor, but another guest heard the noise and reported them, and we were called by the front desk. By the time we got there the individual was gone."

"Was there more than one person?"

"No, just one was spotted, but we don't know if he was alone or with someone."

"Do you know when he came in? Is there video?"

"We haven't had time to look at it yet. There are some cameras in the main lobby, aimed at the check-in desk, and they capture most of that part of the lobby and the elevators."

"But he wasn't able to get into the room?"

"No, someone on the hall had been awake and heard him trying to get into the room by prying open the door. The guest stepped into the hallway. The intruder stopped what he was doing and ran at the guest and knocked the guest down and then went down the emergency stairwell. By the time the guest got up and into the room to call the front desk, which took a few moments to answer, the man was gone. We had a car drive around all of the nearby streets to see if we could find a vehicle that might have brought the person, but our officer didn't see anything. And no one on foot."

"Thanks for calling me. I'll get dressed and come in now. I'd like to talk to the guest while all of this is still fresh on his mind."

"It's a her."

"What?"

"The guest is a woman, not a guy. I thought I said."

"Maybe I missed it. Okay, thanks. I'll be in shortly."

Kathryn was wide awake listening to the conversation. They could also hear Marta moving around in her room. "So, a fire at the shop and someone trying to get into Marta's room, I assume?"

"Looks like it. Two things pretty close together in time in two different places. So at least two people, or he set the fire and then rushed over here. But there were two at her house, so I'm guessing two here. I want to go talk to the woman who spotted the intruder. Will you be okay?"

"Do you think they're likely to come out here? They must know who you are by now?"

"I don't think so. They probably think Marta was in the room. I don't know if they came for her or for information. They won't want to get caught, so they should lie low for now. But I'll call Roddy and have him send someone out here until I get back. He has cars out in the area now."

"I'll feel better if you do."

Redd went into the kitchen and called the county dispatcher and told him what he needed. There was a car six minutes away at the edge of town. He would have the car come to Kathryn's and wait there until he was back. Redd went back to the bedroom and dressed quickly, then knocked on the guest room door and told Marta what had happened. She wanted to come with him, but he refused.

A few minutes later, the deputy's car pulled into the driveway. Redd put on his winter jacket and went out to talk to him, then reset the alarms and left for Staunton.

43

Quite Brave and Quite Lucky

The woman who had been knocked down by the intruder was a slightly overweight, but cute and feisty, representative for a pharmaceutical company. She was about five-seven or maybe five-eight in Redd's quick estimation. She had a bump on her head and a scrape on her cheek from being pushed into the doorframe as the intruder ran past her, but otherwise she was just slightly sore from the fall. She had on a pair of tight exercise pants, which seemed to be the only size those exercise clothes came in these days, to Redd's eye, and a oversized sweatshirt with the company logo on it. Her short hair had been combed into place.

She was seated in the manager's office along with the night desk clerk, a hotel manager who had been called in from home, and a police officer who stood by the wall. The guest's name was JoAnne McBride, and she was pissed off.

"Are you the person in charge?" she asked, as Redd was introduced. "These moron's act like I'm the one who did something here."

The officer spoke. "I was just saying to her that it would have been better for her not to have confronted the person, and to have gone back in her room and called the front desk."

"That's the problem with this country—no one steps up. He might have broken in and raped someone," she said breathlessly.

Redd held up his hand to quiet them both. "Your action was admirable, but the officer is right, you could have been seriously hurt or worse. Fortunately, that didn't happen. But I'd like to just have a few minutes of your time and have you describe what you heard and, more importantly, tell me everything you can about the appearance of the intruder. We might be able to locate him since this just happened."

"Yes, I see, yes. Well, I still can't tell you much. Dressed in black, taller than me, black hair, or dark hair, the hall is a bit dim, you know. He had on a ski mask thing."

"I was afraid that might be the case," said Redd, glancing at the others.

"Why? Who is this person? A terrorist?" asked JoAnne.

"No, not that I know of. Just someone we've been looking for. I can't tell you more than that. What else do you remember? A smell, a sound, his voice?"

"It happened pretty fast."

"Well, tell me from the beginning. Why did you even look out the door? What did you hear?"

"I was awake, anyway. I never sleep well the first night out on these trips. And I hear this scratching noise. At first, I thought it was a bird on the windowsill, but then I realized it was coming from the hall, so I looked out and there he was at the door right over from me. He turned when he heard my door open, and I saw he had this chisel or little crowbar thing in his hand. I just said something like, 'Hey! What are you doing?'—like it just came out. And he ran at me and shoved me, and I fell back into the room after hitting the door frame. The door shut, and then I heard him running down the hall and a door opening, which I guess was the fire escape. I called the front desk."

"You were quite brave and quite lucky," said Redd, without thinking. It was a miracle that the man had not hit her in the head with the crowbar, which would've likely killed her, or had not shot her with a gun he most certainly would have been carrying. Redd quickly realized he was not likely to learn much of value if the intruder was masked and was only seen for seconds.

"Was he wearing gloves?" asked Redd.

"Yeah, black ones, I think. I saw them when he shoved me."

"Anything distinctive about them?'

"No, but they were kind of rough, like cheap leather or something."

"Anything else?"

"No, not really. But you mentioned smell, and there was something different, but I'm not sure what. I can't place it. Maybe it will come to me."

"You mean like a smoke or cigarette smell, or food smell?"

"Yeah, maybe smoke, but different, like a really strong smelly tobacco. I don't know."

"Okay, thanks," said Redd. And he turned to the officer who was standing there. "Could I get you to take her statement, write it all down and send it to me at the FBI number on this card? Then we can let Mrs. McBride go back to her room."

"Miss—it's Miss McBride."

"Of course, I apologize, and I'm sorry for this to have happened."

"It seems to me like you were expecting something like this," she said. "You don't seem surprised." Redd was impressed by her assessment of the situation.

"Not really," replied Redd. "There have been some unusual movements in the area, and we have been on alert for certain individuals."

"That sounds like bullshit to me. Are there terrorists?"

"No, miss, nothing like that. I can't say more than that. But if you use social media, I would appreciate you not calling attention to this incident if possible. I know that may be difficult."

"I'll see. Can I leave now? I have a big day today."

"As soon as the officer takes down your statement."

Redd thanked all of them and went out to his truck. He left a message for Berry and headed back to the farm.

44

Clearly Dead

As soon as he left Staunton his phone buzzed. It was Kathryn. "Redd, you need to get back here right away. There is a strange black SUV up at the big house. I can see it on the screen, the one that shows the camera up there."

"Oh crap. Tell the officer outside—no, I'll call Roddy. Get the rifle out of the gun case."

"How far away are you?"

"Five minutes. Is Marta up?"

"She's right here. Wait…" There was a conversation in the background. Redd had floored the pickup and had his phone on speaker in the truck. "Marta overheard me, she wants me to give her a rifle, too. She says she can shoot."

"Keep me on the phone and go get them then." Redd called Roddy on the two-way radio he kept in his truck. He told him what was going on, and Roddy patched in the officer who was at the farm.

"What should I do?" he asked.

"I'm sending backup right now," said Roddy. "Put the car crossways in the road just up from the house and get behind it. They may have automatic weapons. Go!"

Redd could hear the officer's car start up. A blocked road would give them more time.

"Kathryn, what's happening? Is the SUV still up at the house?"

"It's just sitting there. No, it's backing up now. It maybe is going to ram the gate. I've unlocked the gun cabinet. Marta knows how to handle a rifle. She's loading the Winchester now. I have the bigger one. We're going upstairs. Hold on, the SUV is backing out. It must be coming here now. Hurry!"

Redd was now only about two miles away and driving as fast as he could on the winding road.

He still hadn't heard a siren from any backup Roddy might be sending. It would take the SUV less than half a minute to drive from the big house down to Kathryn's house. Redd was both terrified and angry at himself which pushed him to drive as fast as the conditions would allow. He had gone over 100 miles per hour for a short stretch.

As he topped the hill leading down to the turn, he saw the black SUV approach the sheriff deputy's car. The SUV came to a quick stop, and two men jumped out and pulled some sort of long guns from the rear seat and started firing at the car. They were close enough that if they turned the weapons on the house, the women would not have a chance from any of the front rooms. There was a break in the firing, and Redd could see the officer fire from behind the car and then duck. The two men ducked behind the open doors of the SUV. The one on the right, who was better protected, reached around the door and fired at the officer's car again. At almost the same moment two shots rang out, and the man by the driver's side, who had been leaning around to fire, suddenly jerked upward and then fell. The one on the right stepped around the car and tried to take cover behind the front of the SUV, but the moment his head rose, Redd saw a burst of red, and he fell back.

Redd was turning into the road as the last shot took place, and he nearly lost control in the turn. He gunned the car and slid to a stop pulling a pistol from beneath the seat. Neither of the men was moving, but he approached them with care. The second one was clearly dead, the top of his head blown away. The other one was leaning against the door frame with blood coming from his mouth. He had been shot in the chest and stomach. His eyes were open but seeing nothing. In addition to the strong smell of blood from the wounds, there was a smoky, almost rancid odor coming from the man's jacket. This would almost certainly be the man from the hotel.

Redd called to the officer, who did not respond. He looked to the house as Kathryn and Marta came running from down the short driveway. "Redd, the officer is shot! Call an ambulance!"

Redd hurried around the car, but an ambulance would not be needed. The officer had been hit numerous times in the chest, the bullets passing through the car or bouncing off of the engine block or some other hard metal part in the car. His chest was stained with blood, as was his back where some of the bullets had passed through him.

At that point Redd heard the sirens of approaching cars and turned to the women, who were now standing beside him, each still holding a rifle.

45

Two Assailants

Sheriff Rodabaugh, Roddy, arrived a few minutes later and took charge of the investigation. Marta and Kathryn gave him their weapons and explained that Marta had aimed at the man on the right of the truck and had made the shot that blew the top of his head off. Kathryn had shot the one on the left. They had positioned themselves at two upstairs windows, and with the lights off in the house and the early morning rays of sunlight illuminating the truck and the officer's car, they had had a great sniper's vantage point. Redd knew Kathryn could shoot, but didn't realize how well, and Marta was a complete surprise.

They would both go to the sheriff's office and make a written statement later, as would Redd.

The dead officer was examined and his body loaded into an ambulance. He had only joined the force three months earlier, was twenty-eight, and engaged to be married in three months.

The sun had just been rising when the gun battle took place, and a later investigation would suggest that the officer had been partially blinded by the sun and not able to see the two assailants clearly.

The dead attackers had passports from Albania and some sort of international driver's licenses that would have passed muster if they had been stopped for speeding. The vehicle was rented, and they each had a Visa charge card. There was an Airbnb contract in the vehicle's glove compartment showing an address between Waynesboro and Charlottesville. Redd called Berry and reached him this time, and told him what had happened and chastised him as much as he could get away with for not providing more help up to this point. It was agreed that the FBI would examine the house, pick up the vehicle, and take charge of the bodies of the two assailants.

When all of the procedures around processing the scene had been taken care of, and a time set for Kathryn and Marta's statements, Redd and the two women went into the house.

Both Kathryn and Marta had maintained their composure through the investigation outside, but once away from the activity, they were both distraught over the killing of the deputy.

"Redd," said Marta, grabbing his arm as she spoke, "I should have just stayed at the hotel, or gone somewhere else, and then this wouldn't have happened. It's my fault, and now that poor man is dead."

"Marta," replied Redd, "you and Kathryn most likely saved both your life and hers this morning. And the officer, as sad and tragic as this is, is sworn to protect human lives. We all always knew the risk."

"That doesn't help," said Marta. "My family brought this on, my stupid husband and equally stupid son, now. I'm really sorry, and I want to do whatever I can for the family."

"There will be time for that later. But I have a question, where did you learn to shoot like that? That was incredibly accurate and especially a human target and one with a weapon. That's not easy. Kathryn, I knew you could shoot, I've seen it, but you were both remarkable. Better than some of our deputies used to be."

Kathryn spoke first. "I was thinking about my life, and my life with you and of Marta as well. I've seen some death, as you know, and I hate the people who prey on others. It was me or them. I made objects of them."

"I just thought about my son, dumb as he is, and about the immediate danger, and how not to die. I wasn't as noble as Kathryn here. I didn't have time to think beyond staying alive. I had seen what they did to my house, and they just up and started shooting at that poor man."

"But you both stayed focused. That is an amazing feat."

"I don't think I could have responded in the same way if their guns had been pointed at me," said Kathryn. "This was different, it wasn't like killing a real human. I need to think about it."

"I can get you both some counseling," said Redd. "It's a common practice after a police shooting. It comes back to affect you later."

"I'm okay now," said Kathryn, "but this isn't the end of it, is it? Won't someone come looking for them and find us?"

"Oh God," said Marta, who started to cry. "I hadn't thought of that. Will I ever be safe again?"

Kathryn embraced her. "You will be safe. You'll be protected. Redd?"

"We can put you somewhere safe. I had already requested that, until we can figure out what happened with your son and husband. These men came here to find something, and clearly didn't. I don't know what value there would be in sending someone else and running the risk of exposure. We will have to see what we find when we examine where the men were staying and what communications they may have had with a handler or whomever they were working for. The FBI is getting on that now."

"So, what do we do now?" asked Kathryn.

"I had begun some steps with Wendell. Marta, if you're up to it, I'd like to have you work with him if he can get the CCTV for London, and see if you can spot your husband or son on any of the feeds. I want to take another stab at credit card usage, maybe under a different name, and I need Douglas for that. I also should have thought about this earlier, but the FBI can go to Interpol who can go to the airlines in Europe and find out how the tickets were paid for, and that could give us a card number to work with. I'd start with the Chunnel Train, but the British have the worst systems I've ever worked with. Except for the CCTC. Maybe that's where all the money went. But for now, if you two want to take showers, I'll make coffee."

46

It's All Over Now

Redd ground some coffee beans. He realized his hands were shaking as the scenes from the morning flashed back at him. He wondered what Kathryn's reaction would be once the dust settled. The events, the danger she and Marta had been in, mostly, or entirely due to him and his work. The choices he'd made.

Criminals bringing their threats to the doorstep of law enforcement officials was something that happened only on television shows, not in real life. At least not in the US. In other parts of the world, poverty and corruption provoked a different set of actions. Here, he had never worried about that, not even when he sent convicted killers or violent offenders to prison. Not one of them had ever threatened him when they were released or paroled.

But this was different. He had to assume that the two men were either looking for something—drugs, money, some small but valuable asset—or they were looking for Marta. He couldn't believe they would be looking for Tom or Nathan. Something one or both of them had done had set this in motion. He needed to talk to Marta and unravel the past few months and see if they were missing something. In the meantime, maybe the two dead men would provide some clues as to where to look for the husband and son.

Redd could hear Kathryn on her phone in their bedroom and was about to go and ask her about helping with the chores and managing the cowboys when his phone buzzed. It was the attorney from Charlottesville.

"This is Redd, what's up? I'm going to be tied up for a bit."

"I just saw something on social media, and then we heard something on the radio. A gun battle? Jeez, are you and Kathryn okay?"

"Yeah, we're fine. It's all over now. What's up on your end? I'm afraid I haven't had a chance to look into your guy and the missing woman."

"I understand. It's just that something came up that may shed some light on motive, or motive for revenge, depending on what really happened. There was a post—well, wait—you saw the earlier stuff, right? The crap that was out there?"

"Yeah, I heard about it," said Redd.

"Well, that got a lot of attention, and someone posted that maybe Celia—not named exactly, but identifiable—was setting Dunbar up for having roofied her sister and causing her eventual suicide."

"Is that true? Did you ask him about it?"

"Not yet. I just saw it this morning."

"Didn't you say you had an assistant looking into some of this stuff?"

"Yes, he's the one who saw this post. He responded asking for more details pretending to be a person in the know. He wanted to go further, but that would be a kind of entrapment, and I didn't allow it."

"I don't see how that fits with suspecting Dunbar might have killed her," said Redd. "I mean unless she threatened to expose him, if he did it, and ruin his career, or his marriage, or something else. What did your guy find about her finances? Does she have money troubles? Is it possible the demand for the hundred thousand was real?" Redd asked.

"It looks like she is fine financially. The tech firm is a big player, and she appears to be worth a few million, some of it from the divorce settlement. Money is not an issue, I don't think. No kids, parents and only sister dead, so no immediate relatives needing either financial or personal help. My guy has a list of acquaintances and friends or former friends but hasn't had a chance to pursue them yet. He's going out to Sacramento later today. We had another emergency issue arise, and with Dunbar out on bail, we had to delay it a bit. I also wanted to talk to you first and see how you wanted to handle it. I imagine you can't think about that right now though."

"I really can't give it much attention for a day or two. Have your guy talk to as many friends of both of them as he can find, especially friends from their college days. I assume that's when this occurred. Find out all you can. And as much about the sister as possible as well. And of course, ask Dunbar first and see what he says."

"That was going to be the first thing this morning after talking to you. I'll let you know. Let me know when you have a break. My best to Kathryn."

They clicked off.

47

Antibiotic Shots

O ther than wanting some coffee, no one felt like eating anything that morning. Marta went along with Kathryn to help with the morning chores but really to just do something that was outdoors, safe, and in many ways affirming, something as basic and ordinary as chores that contributed eventually to feeding people. Redd went to the far pasture to help two of the cowboys move pregnant cows to another field. They didn't really need his help, but he had the same need to be away from the house and the blood of two violent criminals. The bodies and the car had been taken away, and a fire truck had come and washed the road clear of blood and debris, and there was no evidence now that anything out of the ordinary had taken place, but Redd would never pass that spot by the front of the house and not be reminded of all he might have lost that day.

After chores, Redd met Kathryn and Marta back at the small vet barn where there were several calves that still needed treatment, and Redd helped Kathryn work them through the chute to hold them steady for antibiotic shots, since the oral treatments didn't seem to be helping. Kathryn had called the school and told them she would be out for the day and her teaching assistant would take over. Redd had met her assistant, a brilliant young woman who had already been cited on papers and been awarded several prizes for her work as a student. Kathryn had supervised her early efforts and asked her to be her assistant as soon as she felt the young woman was ready.

Redd proposed that if Marta was up to it, they do an online connection with Berry and see if she could see any of the CCTV footage from London that Berry was now accessing. It would be a sort of diversion for her.

48

Clearly Visible

The attack by the Albanians had given Berry and a part of his team the push needed to pay some attention to Marta's case. By the time the two women and Redd were back in the house, Berry had managed to set up a link with a cohort in London who was ready to work with Marta when she could give them some addresses to access.

From the earlier credit card information, she had the name of the hotel and the right dates.

They began looking at coverage starting an hour and a half after her son's plane would have landed. He would have taken the Heathrow Express to Paddington, a trip that took only twenty minutes if there were no delays. Arrivals in the new Queen's terminal were fairly efficient with the new automatic screening of face and passport, but it was a long walk, up to two miles, from the arrival gate to the station deep underground for the subway and express trains.

They were looking at December 19, late morning arrival time. The plane should have landed at 9:00, so 11:00 London time. At 11:30 Marta spots a young man getting out of a London taxi who she believes is her son. His face is never completely clear, but the roller bag, which is an expensive silver one, and the backpack, with a pair of white tennis shoes—or trainers, as the British call them—dangling from the side, a habit of his which annoys her.

They are able to pick him up inside on a camera in the lobby of the hotel. Here he was clearly visible. It was too early to check-in, so he left his roller bag and his trainers with a porter and kept the backpack. He was seen going off to one side where the camera didn't have a field of vision, presumably a toilet or hallway. He reappeared about fifteen minutes later and took a seat in a lounge-like area across from and to the side of the lobby. A few minutes later a man appeared and sat down in a chair at a ninety-degree angle from Nathan. They acknowledged each other but didn't shake hands. Then they could be seen talking. The expressions on both faces, to the extent that could be seen, showed signs of consternation and concern. Nathan could be seen gesturing in a way that would indicate puzzlement. He shook his head from side to side, raised his arms with the palms open and turned up, a classic questioning pose. The other man gestured with a raised first finger, chastising, questioning, indicating.

After about five minutes of this interchange, they both got up and left the area. At this point, Redd asked all parties to pause for a moment.

"Marta," he said, "did you recognize the man Nathan was talking to?"

She thought for a moment. "I don't know. I don't have a really clear memory of the man my husband met on that cruise. This man seems to be the right build, but he is more heavily dressed. It was warmer when we saw him, or whoever it was, and I could get a better sense of size and so on. He was a big guy, like this one. And now that I've seen the two dead guys, or at least the one I didn't shoot, I think his features were a bit like them, you know, Slavic is it called?"

"Russian, perhaps," suggested Berry.

"Maybe," she said. "I told Redd earlier, I didn't think his accent was original English, like he wasn't born there."

"I understand," said Berry. "Unless you were born somewhere or learned the language before age five or so, it's almost impossible not to have some sort of accent, no matter how good your language skills."

"If I could hear him talk, that would help, but I know that's not possible."

They resumed watching, fast forwarded for periods but didn't catch the two of them together again that day in the hotel. They looked at a recording outside and saw the two of them get into a taxi a few minutes after the first meeting indoors, but couldn't read the taxi license number. They reviewed recordings stretching over December 20 but didn't see either person. It was tiring work and a strain on the eyes. They checked the notes that Redd made during his first interview with Marta, and they decided to concentrate on December 21, the day Nathan said he was leaving for Amsterdam. He was seen at 9:00 a.m. checking out and a few minutes later getting into a taxi outside. That is the last they see of him. The only thing they have learned is that he met a man who could have been the same person his father met in England.

It was now close to noon, and after the events of the morning, Marta was tired and so was Redd. Kathryn had gone up to the large house to check on something. He texted her, and she said she would be back in half an hour. Marta went to the guest room and fell asleep almost instantly. Redd sat down in a recliner by the kitchen fireplace and fell asleep as well. He popped awake when Kathryn came in the kitchen door. They warmed some soup and both went to the bedroom to sleep for an hour or two. Marta did not awaken.

49

Thomas McFerren

Berry and his team had continued to watch the CCTV feeds. On December 28, Tom was seen arriving at the same hotel and meeting the same man that Nathan had met a few days earlier. There was a similar conversation with more strain and apparent anger showing in the videos. They departed again as Nathan had done, but later in the day, Tom was seen returning.

The following morning, he checked out and presumably left for the airport for the flight to Amsterdam. This was the last they saw of him.

They were able to confirm where he stayed in the hotel in Amsterdam and finally got back information from the airline where he had used a different credit card, one that Marta has no record of. This could be a treasure trove as Nathan is also on this account, and they can begin to follow more of his movements, assuming he used this card frequently.

Berry pulled the credit card information and sent it along to Redd.

There was now something to work with.

At 5:00 p.m., Berry got an alert from Interpol from the Dutch police that a body had been found in a warehouse near the harbor, and a passport in the jacket pocket has the name Thomas McFerren on it.

Berry sent an encrypted email to Redd, instead of calling him. This was turning into a tough day for Marta Miller.

50

Bad News

It was after eight when Redd next checked his email. They had driven into town and eaten at a small wine bar that had expanded to light meals with a French theme. People recognized them from the news of the shootout that was constantly being reviewed on the various channels. The fact that the two women had killed the Albanians was headlines and had been picked up by CNN and other national networks. Roddy had kept the roads closed and officers stationed in the area. Reporters had not been able to get to any of the three to ask questions or interview them, but drone views of the farm and Kathryn's house were now being shown constantly. The woman who ran the wine bar took them to a back corner so that they could at least have a small degree of privacy.

They returned to the house after dinner. Redd started a fire in the kitchen fireplace and then motioned to Kathryn to meet him in the bedroom. Marta settled into a loveseat by the fire while Redd discreetly told Kathryn what he had learned about Tom McFerren.

"I need to tell her about it right now," he said, "but this is so much on top of this morning. How do I handle it?"

"You just handle it. You just tell her. I'll help however I can. I think she's expecting it, but…"

"I know. Expecting and knowing are two different things."

They left the room and went out to chairs by the fire.

"Marta," said Redd, "I have some bad news."

"Not Nathan, don't tell me it's Nathan," she replied immediately, looking from Redd to Kathryn, as if beseeching her to protect her from the news.

"No, it's your husband, Tom. They've found a body in Rotterdam, and his passport was in a pocket, so on that basis they are assuming that it is really him. There will need to be further verification. I'm really sorry."

Tears sprang to her eyes, and Kathryn went to her and sat beside her on the loveseat and took her in her arms. "I am sorry, Marta, really sorry."

Marta wiped away the tears and breathed in and was quiet for a few moments.

"I am not surprised in a way, in spite of what I said about thinking he was not dealing with dangerous people. You can't just keep cheating people and not make some serious enemies. This is terrible to say, but I was growing to hate him, hate him for what he was, and hate him for what he had done to my son, what he had turned him into. And hating myself for letting it happen."

"There is no good time for such news, but this is a tough day to hear it," said Redd.

"No, not really," said Marta. "I feel like I maybe partially avenged it by shooting that son of a bitch's head off today. Where did they find him—Tom, I mean?"

"I don't have a lot of detail yet, but in Rotterdam in a warehouse. I don't know any more than that."

"But no news about Nathan?"

"No, sorry, not so far. We know from the videos that Tom met with the same guy in London and then went on to

Amsterdam like he said. And what he texted about Florence seems to be born out. We have a different credit card and more information on dates and where he stayed.

Someone is checking those locations now to see if they can learn anything more that might help find Nathan."

"I want to go look for him," said Marta, jumping up from her chair. "I want to go find him."

"Marta," said Redd, "that won't help. And it's dangerous. You need to let the FBI and the European police do this."

"Redd, until you got involved, no one was taking any real interest in this. How excited do you think they are about looking for the killer of a con man? And I'm sure they have all that information about Tom right now. They know his reputation. And with Nathan working with him, they're going to think the same."

"No, I don't agree. Marta, the Dutch police deal with international crime all the time. Amsterdam is a major hub. They will put resources on this."

"What if Nathan isn't in Amsterdam or Rotterdam or anywhere in the Netherlands any longer, then who's going to go looking? Who's looking in Florence? Or back in London maybe?"

"Marta, let me get the full picture in the morning, and then I can tell you more accurately what's going on, who's looking for Nathan, and how it's being organized. And yes, I know things should have started earlier. We were thrown off by the attack at your place."

"Alright, but you can't stop me from going if I want to go, can you?" she said defiantly.

"No, we can't, but I would really, really advise against that."

"You could come with me."

"Marta!" said Kathryn, but before she could say more, Marta burst into tears and turned to Kathryn and mumbled that she was sorry.

After a moment Marta said, "I didn't mean that, and that was unkind. You've protected me, and I'm being ungrateful. I'm sorry. I'll just go to bed now."

She got up, and when Redd stood up, she went to him and hugged him and said thanks and then walked down the hall to the guest room.

"I can't imagine," said Kathryn. "I mean, I lost my father in a violent way, but losing a husband, even one you might not love so much anymore, has to be tough, and fearing that your son may be dead as well is probably as tough as it gets."

"Pretty close to it, I'd think," replied Redd. "I need to talk to Wendell to see what all they have learned, but it will have to be in the morning."

They checked the doors and turned down the lights and headed for bed.

Redd held Kathryn close as they fell asleep, and it seemed like only moments later, they were awakened by a light tapping at their door. "Marta, is that you?" asked Kathryn, who had woken more quickly than Redd.

"Yes. Can I come in?"

"Of course, I'll turn on a light."

"No, don't. It's just that I can't sleep. I'm really scared. I just, I just…"

"It's fine. I'll slide over a bit, and you can get in next to me here. It's fine."

Marta was dressed in a long winter nightgown, and she slid into the bed beside Kathryn who had turned on her side with her back to Redd. Kathryn put her right arm over Marta and held her until they both fell asleep.

51

Interpol

Redd had slept relatively well in spite of the crowded bed and all that had occurred the day before and woke up around six as usual. He made a pot of coffee and went to his office to see if Berry had sent anything more to him overnight.

There was a good summary of what they had found. McFerren had not been dead long, no more than forty-eight hours. The weather had been unusually cold, so deterioration was minimal. There was a photo of the face that they would need Marta to identify, but it matched the one in the passport found in his coat pocket.

The fact that identification was found on the body seemed to indicate that the killers wanted it to be known that McFerren was dead. The question was who might the recipient of the message be? Nathan? That made no sense. So, it was either a message to someone else involved in the drug chain, if that was truly what this was, or a warning.

The warehouse was not an abandoned one, as he had somehow assumed, but one that was used for trans-shipments. Unfortunately, that didn't provide any more of a clue either.

McFerren had no other documents in his pockets.

But the airline had provided the credit card number for the purchase of tickets, and they now had a list of the hotels, restaurants, and flights that both he and Nathan had taken.

Redd looked first at the charges that applied to Tom McFerren. These charges picked up with the Chunnel train that had brought him to Amsterdam, where he had stayed two nights—as he had reported to Marta—then he had flown to Florence, presumably on the tracks of Nathan, where he must not have located him, because he then flew back to Amsterdam after two nights and only a full day in Florence and took a train from Amsterdam to Rotterdam. This was on January second. He had booked a hotel there, and there were restaurant charges for the second, third, and fourth of January, but no food charges after the morning of the fourth. But there was no indication that he had checked out of the hotel. It was now January ninth, and he had presumably been killed on the sixth or seventh. If he had not checked out, perhaps there would be documents or something at the hotel to help explain his actions.

Redd then looked at the charges for Nathan. Nathan had arrived in London on the nineteenth of December and stayed there for two nights only before going on to Amsterdam on the twenty-first. He had stayed at a small hotel on the outskirts of the city for two nights. He checked out on the twenty-third and went to Rotterdam for three days where he spent Christmas Eve and Christmas Day in a dreary little hotel near an industrial part of the city. On the twenty-sixth, he checked out and took a train back to Amsterdam and flew to Nice where he stayed one night, and on the twenty-seventh, he flew in the afternoon to Paris where he stayed one night again. Finally, on the twenty-eighth he flew from Paris to Florence and checked into a hotel for one night. He had also used several cash machines to pull out the maximum cash withdrawals allowed on the charge card, almost six thousand euros. He then disappeared.

Due to the probability of drugs being smuggled and the citizenship of the victim, Interpol, the European investigation group, had taken control of the situation and would send another report at the end of their day, five or six hours from the current time. From the travel itinerary that Redd had seen, he was glad that Interpol was handling the case. None of it made sense to him.

52

Traces of Fentanyl

After morning chores and breakfast, Kathryn left for the university and a return to a slightly more normal day.

Redd had talked to her before she left, and he would talk to Marta about what he had learned and see if she could shed any further light on Tom's and Nathan's travels.

Marta was much more composed. She had been able to sleep relatively soundly and even joked to Redd about him spending the night in bed with two women but dropped the subject when he told her not to expect to do that on a regular basis. Marta seemed to have an undercurrent of irrepressible sexuality.

They sat at the table in the kitchen, so that Redd could take notes if needed. He took her through the events in Europe, only a bit of which she knew about. Tom had not confided in her about any conversations he had had with Nathan before leaving for Europe.

"The truth of the matter is that I was away part of the time," said Marta. "I think I told you I was really angry with him, and with Nathan, too, to a lesser degree. I was sick of being in that isolated house, I was tired of being married to a crook, and

I was planning to divorce him, but I wanted to be sure I had access to enough money to tide me over until I could come up with something to do. Graves, the congressman, you know, had promised he could get me a good position with one of the lobbying firms up in DC, but I wasn't sure what that would entail. He's a charming guy, but I don't really trust him. I guess that comes from living with Tom so long."

"I can see how trust gets eroded," said Redd.

"Well, it doesn't apply to you," she replied. "I don't think you've ever done a dishonest thing in your life, have you?"

"I wouldn't go that far," Redd smiled and replied. "Nothing evilly dishonest, though."

"Ha, modesty. Anyway, to get back to Tom, I really wasn't following all he was up to. And I was thinking about it last night—I really don't know what Nathan was up to. He could have gone to Europe ten times in the past year, and unless he mentioned it, I wouldn't have known. He lived—lives—in Charlottesville, you saw the apartment and the shop, but I didn't see him there often and had never been to that little shop. By the way, what's happening with that?"

"We'll go over later if we have time. The damage was less than we thought, especially the one back room, and the TSA guys will take a dog in later. If they find anything, the Charlottesville police will let me know."

"Oh yeah, I kinda forgot about that. So, other than that broad outline of exporting Native American artwork, I really am not sure what either one of them was up to. I know that's not much help, and this is awful to say, but in some ways, I was more interested in finding out where Tom was for my own sake, my own financial sake, and not so much for his. Does that sound awful?"

"Yes and no. I can see how you might want out. I'm surprised you stuck with him as long as you did."

"Inertia, I guess, and the alternatives. Do you have any idea how many losers there are floating around out there? I mean a woman my age is not going to find a bunch of Redd Herrings out there just waiting for someone like me. Or anyone, really. They are all either horny, and wanted some sex with no commitment, or a mother to take care of them, or a therapist to tell them how great their miserable lives are. At least Tom didn't ask questions when I was off having fun, and I didn't have to mother him."

Redd looked at Marta with a puzzled look on his face for a moment. "I guess I understand what you're saying. Kathryn has said a few of the same things. I'm not sure how it got to that. Maybe it always been that way, and no one could see the alternatives. But I have a question. You say you were away a lot and not paying much attention to what Tom was up to. Did he show signs of being worried, or say anything about this project going bad, something not working the way he thought it was supposed to? I mean it looks like whatever they were doing fell apart in a major way very quickly. He must have been concerned."

"Thinking back on it, he was in a bad mood, but I kind of thought it was because I was being a bitch. He did go off for some conversations out of earshot, and he was gone several times for a day or two on business stuff, but never out of the country."

"I see. Well, I'm guessing we'll just have to wait on a report from Interpol to see what they turn up."

Redd was about to ask her about more detail on their finances when his phone rang. It was the Charlottesville police. "This is Redd."

"Good morning. This is Captain Dewey. I have some information for you on the shop on 29. TSA were able to trace cocaine at the shop, and they were also able to detect traces of fentanyl. They have only recently begun to train dogs for that, apparently, but there were definitely traces. They used two different dogs. Does that help you?"

"Yes, that confirms what I feared. Anything else?"

"No, we didn't find anything else. We were lucky that there were several almost airtight closets at the rear, and the fire didn't reach those areas, and even the smoke hadn't penetrated greatly. I doubt if the dogs would have been able to detect anything if it had been worse."

"This is all helpful. I appreciate your help. I won't need to come back over now."

He clicked off and told Marta what he had learned.

"That bastard. Drugs. So dangerous. I'm not totally sorry he's dead. But I am terrified for Nathan now. God help him." She stood and walked back to the guest bedroom and closed the door.

53

One More Question

Redd called Berry, who answered on the first ring for a change, and told him what the dogs had found at the shop.

"I'm not surprised. The Interpol guys in Rotterdam sent me a note a bit ago. They've been working with the local authorities, and they've picked up through informants that something fairly big went down a few weeks ago. There's an import agent who went missing and so did a lot of inventory. It looks like the agent may have been the guy McFerren was working with. They've just gotten into the import agent's office but expect to be able to tell me something in the next day or so."

"Crap. That reminds me—there was an import agent's name in the material we found at Nathan's apartment, or in the shop. I thought I sent that on to you, but with all that's been happening here, I'm not sure I did. Was it in the stuff I scanned and sent? Damn. I'll bet the name matches."

"I'll double-check. I don't know that McFerren could have gotten to the agent anyway, and McFerren has been missing or dead a few days. I'll look again. It's probably in there. Only important if it doesn't match the name we're looking for now," said Berry.

"So, what does what you have now mean? Was the missing agent into drug smuggling? I guess no one would know, would they?" asked Redd.

"Who knows what the Rotterdam police or Interpol may have known."

"One more question. Relative to these pieces, what does this mean immediately, then?"

"Well, on the surface, it might mean that the product McFerren was sending over might have gone missing, and if that's the case, then whoever was expecting it will want their money or the product back. It's as simple as that."

"Okay, that would explain a lot—why they sent goons here to look for it, and why both Tom and Nathan went to try to locate it, I presume."

"Since Tom got killed," said Berry, "that must mean he didn't find it, or couldn't pay up."

"Which means Nathan is either dead or in a world of trouble."

"I would vote for Nathan being on the run, based on the limited info we have. The cash withdrawal was his attempt to go dark and not leave a trail."

"That's not that easy in Europe, is it?" asked Redd.

"It's not that easy anywhere, anymore," replied Berry. "He disappeared in Florence, but I'm guessing he would want to get out of there as fast as possible. It's an expensive city. And he might have been followed. We just don't know."

"What's your next step?"

"Interpol has put out alerts. In the meantime, they're searching the hotel room where Tom stayed. And combing thru any informants to see if they can get more details. You'll just have to sit tight."

Redd clicked off and found Marta had come back out of the room.

"I heard a little bit of what you were saying. You think Nathan is dead too?"

"No, it was just a concern. Berry thinks he's on the run from Florence. Interpol is searching for him."

"I see. Do you think you could take me back to my house? I didn't bring much with me, and I need some changes of clothes. I'm not sure where I should go next. I guess back to the hotel? Is that safe now?"

"It probably is, but you're welcome to stay here for a few days."

"I appreciate that, but I think I just need to be alone for a bit."

"I have another matter I need to spend a bit of time on. Let me see if I can get Roddy to send an officer to take you down to the house and bring you back to the hotel."

"That would be very kind of you, Redd. Thank you."

Forty-five minutes later, one of Roddy's officers, a young woman who had been on the force for three years, drove up and picked up Marta, who took along her backpack and the clothes she had brought from the hotel just two days earlier. She promised to check in with Redd when she was back at the hotel.

54

Dawson

The attorneys for Gabe Dunbar had been sorting through the social media posts. Their research-investigator associate, Dawson Troop, had finally flown to Sacramento and met with the local police who let him into Sandy's apartment. It was a furnished apartment, and the manager of the complex told him Sandy had told him that she wanted to rent it on a short-term basis while she looked for a house to buy. Sacramento had a number of such units that legislators and lobbyists would rent when they needed to be in town for an extended period of time. The unit was quite elegant for a furnished apartment, furnished more like an Airbnb or rental by owner, with high-end linens and a quality assortment of dishes and cookware.

Dawson was surprised to find very few of Sandy's clothes in the closets, and assumed she must be storing furniture and clothing from her married life somewhere else. There were a few old pairs of sneakers and some exercise outfits, sweatshirts and a few sweaters, older underwear and socks.

There were a few restaurant and grocery store receipts in the kitchen drawers, but no personal files, no mail, a limited number of hand creams. The manager told him she had only been there for the past six weeks, so he supposed that explained the lack of toiletries and cosmetics he would have expected to find in the bathroom. But it struck him strange that there were no feminine products like tampons or panty liners, things his own wife always kept a supply of. It almost seemed like Celia had left with no intention of coming back.

His next step was to find people who had known the sister who had died. Her name was Julia, and she had been born two years after Sandy. With the parent's being dead and Sandy missing, he had no close relative to turn to, but Facebook turned out to be a better personal information source than any amount of research in the past. He soon found out that she had been living in LA at the time of her death, had gradually shunned or ghosted what friends she had had, and toward the end, if the posts were to be believed, had fallen into a deep depression and taken an overdose of a drug cocktail and ended her life. Most of the posts came from two women who still lived in LA, one of them a small-time actress, single and pretty with a whirlwind social life—if her daily posts were to be believed. The other was a divorced blond who posted about women's rights and social justice on a regular basis. Both women had known Julia in college and had apparently tried to be her support group.

Dawson was five years out of law school and found that he liked day-to-day research and background work better than the more technical application of legal principles. He had gotten married right after receiving his degree, and he and his wife Adele had a three-year-old daughter named Mollie. Adele was in her eighth month of a second pregnancy.

Dawson was adept at social media, knew the ins and out of all of the platforms and could track his way back to individuals through the information they listed freely on the web or social sites. The law firm also subscribed to databases, and it had not been difficult to find the addresses and phone numbers for the two friends in LA. He had arranged to meet them the following day.

Dawson had just arrived at the Sacramento airport for a flight on Southwest down to LA when his phone rang with the distinctive ring he had set up for his wife. "Dawson, honey, where are you?" she asked.

"Hi. I'm just about to get on a plane from Sacramento to LA. What's up?"

"I really need you to come home, I'm sorry, but Mollie has a fever and has been throwing up for hours, and the sitter won't stay with her because she's afraid she'll catch it. I really shouldn't be carrying Mollie around, she's too heavy, and I certainly can't risk catching whatever crud she has at this stage. I'm sorry."

Neither of their parents lived near them, and Dawson knew there was no one else she could call at the moment. Her mother would come when the baby was born, but they couldn't ask her to come for this.

"Oh geez, let me see what I can do. I don't know what connections I can get out of here. Hopefully I can get close. It might be morning unless I can get something through Salt Lake or Denver to Richmond maybe. Let me call the office."

When he reached the receptionist she transferred him to the office manager, and between them they found a flight leaving in an hour that would connect in Denver and get him into Richmond close to midnight. It was the best he could do. He called his wife back and told her what he had booked. He then called the office once again and talked to Lawrence Luther, his partner, and told him what he had found and what was happening at home. Luther decided he would call Redd and see if he could fly out to LA and do the interview with the two women. He hoped things had calmed down for Redd by now.

55

Bad Joke

As soon as he finished the call with Dawson, Luther called Herring. It was midafternoon. Redd answered the call.

"Redd, I need you to do something for me," said Luther. "Oh, sorry—hi, how are you?"

Redd laughed. "You must have trained with the guy I work with at the FBI—he's not into conventional niceties like hello and goodbye."

Lawrence laughed. "I apologize. I just got off another call, and my mind was on a track. How are things with you by the way? A few exciting and dangerous days."

"I'll say, but I think that danger in the US is now gone. Not sure, but I hope so. There are other developments."

"How is Kathryn, and how is your client? That was that hot woman who was with you when we first met, wasn't it? She was a looker."

"Yes, that was her. I had no idea she was that good with a rifle. Said she went to shooting ranges, and she obviously has a steady hand and a good eye."

"Maybe her husband didn't disappear in Europe after

all—did you think of that? No, no. Sorry, I shouldn't have said that. Bad joke."

"You wouldn't know, but he was found dead in Amsterdam yesterday."

"Oh jeez, that was really insensitive of me. Sorry, sorry, sorry."

"No problem. But what did you need from me?"

"Okay, I have a researcher in Sacramento who was headed to LA to interview two women who knew the woman who disappeared and knew the sister who died by suicide, and he was on the way to see them and had to come back for a family health crisis. His wife is pregnant, and their first kid is sick, and it can't be avoided. I hate to lose the momentum on this, and time is of the essence. Is there any chance you could pop out there and interview the two women for me? I don't have anyone else I can send."

"I might be able to. Let me check with Kathryn. It would have to be tomorrow at the earliest, and I would want to do a quick roundtrip on this. Have you had anyone check flights?"

"No, but I will, and I'll text you. I'll book you in First Class if you agree."

"I'm getting used to that, unfortunately. I'll let you know as soon as I talk to Kathryn and make sure everything is secure here and nothing is needed for the Europe investigation."

56

Albanians, Not Russians

Redd had heard a vehicle drive up as he clicked off the call, and through the window he could see Douglas's old pickup pulling into the drive. He was glad to see him, and he knew Kathryn would be too. And since it was this late, Douglas would stay overnight. He and Kathryn had wanted to go out to see him for the last several days, but the other events had obviously prevented that.

He wanted to fill Douglas in on the developments in Europe and see if he could add anything new to the work he had already done, or to what the police in Rotterdam had found. Redd hadn't heard whether they had found out anything more about the missing import agent. He wondered if they had been able to access the agent's office and find any records that could help locate Nathan.

He greeted Douglas at the back door and went out to get some firewood for the kitchen fireplace. Douglas came along, and the two of them quickly filled the wood storage area built into the hearth. Redd lit a fire just as Kathryn arrived, and she opened a bottle of Sauvignon Blanc and poured a small glass for herself and Redd and poured Douglas a glass of cider.

"I hear that the barbarians have been at the gate," said Douglas. "The descendants of Genghis Khan and Tamerlane set loose in the west."

"How did you hear about this?" asked Kathryn. "I thought news was a forbidden topic with you."

"Generally speaking it is, but I do know a few people in the little hamlet of Monterey over there, and they speak to me when I'm in town, as hard as that might be to believe. I stopped for gas, and it was mentioned in passing that my sister had been in a gunfight. I thought I better come check it out. I think I told you this guy here would be trouble," nodding toward Redd.

"I should have listened, but I'm stuck with him now," responded Kathryn. "It's more frightening to think about now, but it was very quick when it happened. You probably heard there were two of us involved. Redd's client was pretty handy with a rifle, thank goodness. It might have had a different ending otherwise."

"So, you and that woman really did kill a couple of Russians? I thought it was made up or misinterpreted."

"Not made up, but they were Albanians, not Russians."

"Well, the locals don't know where either place is, so they could have been from Vermont, and it would be just as exotic. Are you okay?"

"Yeah. It might hit me more later, but right now I'm fine with it."

Douglas turned to Redd. "So, I'm guessing this is related to your art theft guys who went missing? Pretty strong response for a giclée or a watercolor, I'd say."

"Yeah, we haven't established the link, but it has to be. And the husband who went missing was found dead in Rotterdam, and he was probably killed a day or two before this attack. The son is still missing."

"You still don't know what they were up to?"

"It almost has to be drugs. Sniffer dogs found scents from cocaine and fentanyl in the shop that the son used, so I'd say he was involved, yes. And it appears that some inventory has gone missing and so is the agent who handled the imports of the artwork for him. Somebody must have stolen some of the merchandise, and somebody else is looking for it."

"Logical. Anything on the computer or records from the agent?"

"Not so far, but I'll send a note to Berry, now that you're here, if you wouldn't mind looking."

Kathryn interrupted. "How's your needlepoint project coming along? I'm still surprised that's complex enough for you."

"The complexity comes from designing your own tapestry. I'm applying a mathematical formula to a color gradation scheme to see what that might produce. I've been thinking of taking a trip to Europe to look at some old tapestries and maybe go to Oudenaarde in Belgium, which was famous for its tapestries back in the twelfth century or so. It might give me a sense of place, a tie to a different skill, even now. Colorful history."

"I'm worried that Redd's FBI friend is going to want to send him to the Netherlands or somewhere else if they don't sort out this missing person business soon. Maybe you could go together, and you could keep him out of trouble."

"No offense, Redd, but not my thing."

57

This Is Sloppy

After a vegetarian dinner, Redd and Douglas went back to his office to check on any updates from Berry. One of the European agencies, probably Interpol with the help of the local authorities, had sent along a summary of the pertinent information from the office of the missing agent in Rotterdam.

The import agent had recently been pegged for greater surveillance based on a tip from an informant in Amsterdam. The basis for the tip was that several killings in that city had been related to competition from an unknown source of cocaine, fentanyl, and several other base chemicals coming into Europe. The South American cartel-funded group wanted it shut down.

The informant had his own little side gig going in non-drug-related items but was tolerated because of the information he could supply and because of his own network of seedy spies.

Unfortunately, the agent had not yet come under surveillance due to higher priority needs, so they had had little to go on except a tip.

On paper, at least, the import agent was a facilitator for importing semi-valuable artwork, a clearing house for mainly more modern and ethnic pieces, such as Native American works like the ones Nathan had purported to sell. Nathan's company in Charlottesville was his primary supplier. And, he seemed to be focusing on a very limited number of clients in Europe, with usually only one location in each of several of the largest cities. There was someone in Florence, the only location in Italy; one each in Bordeaux, Lyon, Paris, and Marseille; six in various German cities; and several others scattered about. There was almost no inventory on hand, but on the computer in his office there were photos of various pieces with different options for framing. The frames were generally quite large and bulky in design, and the ones made from metal would have been hollow. Some of the other frames looked like the designs he and Marta had seen in Charlottesville at Nathan's apartment and shop. It was almost certain that Nathan had been receiving drugs from a source in the US and packing them in the frames, welding them shut or sealing them in custom 3-D printed frames where they could not be smelled or detected. The report stated that no drugs or evidence of drugs was found at the agent's office, so if their hypotheses were correct, the drugs were not removed from the frames until they got to the customers from the shops in each of the cities.

The agent appeared to have contacts in London, but nothing was ever shipped to England, Scotland, or Wales. The shipments were only to the shops on the continent. In the next two days, Interpol would arrange with the police in each of the cities to investigate or raid the shops listed.

Those were the key points in the report, but further down, the report listed a summary of several exchanges that had taken place between the import agent and Nathan. Nathan had been supplied the agent's name almost a year ago. He had initially shipped framed giclées that were just that, framed giclées with no drugs stuffed in the frames. They had been weighted to match the weights that would eventually be the weight of frames containing drugs. It was a trial run, but more, it was to establish a pattern that would not attract attention when the real smuggling began. That process had started in late summer, about the time that Marta reported Tom's meeting with the possible Russian in England.

The videos from the hotel where the meeting occurred had been given to Interpol, and they had identified the man meeting with Tom as a Sergei Blaskoff, who called himself Stephen Baskin in England. He owned a horse farm but was not a member of the British Horse Racing Society, which policed its membership to discourage illegal activity. He had briefly been in a partnership with a Sir Anthony Howe. Scotland Yard had sent someone to visit Blaskoff—Baskin at home—but he was reported to be out of the country. There was a footnote from Berry, that Baskin had been in the US at various times during the past year, but not for the past six months. He had not been flagged, as there were no records of criminal activity for him. He was thought to own an expensive condo in Manhattan through an offshore company. At the time no record of beneficial ownership—or in plain language, who the real owner might be—had been required. That was to change under new laws in the US. But that consideration aside, Baskin could easily have and probably had, connected with Tom McFerren at some point in the US, and that would have been when the scheme was born. Tom's meeting with him in England corresponded with the dates when the real shipments of drugs began.

After they had both read the materials, Redd turned to Douglas. "Why in the world would someone go to the trouble to bring drugs into the US and then take a second chance by exporting them to Europe? Why not just smuggle them to Europe to begin with. The cocaine would have come up from South America and the fentanyl mostly from Mexico?"

"There is a certain cleverness to it, if you think about it. Who would expect drugs to come into Europe from the US? It's pretty safe in many respects. For the smugglers, I mean. And it's another route if one of the established ones gets hit. And maybe it wasn't just cocaine and fentanyl. Could have been some illegal chemicals to make fentanyl or some of the other stuff floating around Europe. Meth maybe, I don't know. But it's also sort of a soft scam on the giclée artists. It almost diverts from the real crime."

"I suppose. I was never involved with drug stuff other than small-time meth labs and some minor possession issues before marijuana was legalized. And I never wanted to be."

"Why not?" asked Douglas.

"I might have mentioned it before, but it was just having to do with the hopelessness of the users in so many cases, but more, it was the incredible violence, especially from the cartels. I didn't want to have that here. And you can see, just in the last two days, these people have no regard for human life at all. I wish I had never been asked to take on this case."

"Do you think you or Kathryn will be in danger in the future? Is she in danger now?" asked Douglas.

"I don't think so, but I don't know for sure. If we can find Nathan, or figure out what the endgame is on what's happening in Europe, find the import agent maybe, then I'll have a better idea. Tom is dead, and he must have set this all up with Nathan. He seems to have been the point man with the English-Russian guy. If this shuts down the scheme, then there's no point in risking attacking me or Kathryn, or probably even Marta, the wife, and drawing attention to yourself. He already lost two men. This is sloppy."

"Do you have any background on the two men who the women shot?"

"I was waiting on a report from Berry—let me check if

there's an update. I was most interested in the stuff we just read. Hold on—yeah, here."

Redd scanned the email from Berry. "Ah, the vehicle was registered in Canada, had stolen US license plates, the two are thought to have come across the border somewhere in North Dakota or Montana, maybe, an unmanned back road. There were prepaid credit cards in their possession, and they kept receipts from gas stations. Someone else rented the house for them, not much else. Info sent to the Canadians to figure out where they came from."

"Well, I hope you're right. Maybe you should take her away from here for a while. She's all I've got. But you know that."

"Yes, and she's all I've got too. I hope you know how important she is to me as well."

Douglas nodded and smiled at him. "Yes, I do. I'm going to go talk to her and give her a hard time now though. Otherwise, she'll think something is wrong with me. And I still won't go to Europe with you."

58

Rachel and Deborah

Redd had forgotten about the call from Lawrence, but when he checked his emails there was a message that had been left an hour or so after Lawrence's call that afternoon:

> Redd, I took the liberty of booking you on a roundtrip to LA from Charlottesville, one night only, Marriott Hotel at the airport in LA. Ten-fifteen departures on both ends. My assistant arranged for the two women our assistant was planning to interview to come to the hotel to meet you. Small conference room reserved if you need it. Plane ticket is refundable and changeable, but I hope you can make it.

There was another email with the flight arrangements—first class seats and a whopping $1,800 price tag. Dunbar would be paying for that. There was also a hotel reservation for a room with a king-size bed at the hotel.

There was one other email, forwarded from Dawson, the research assistant, with the names and contact information of the two women, along with a short note on each.

Deborah Singer was the actress. There was a print of a studio photo attached—wholesome good looks, dark curly hair, looked like the kind of spokesperson one would see for a car or cell service or as a supporting actress in some family comedy.

Rachel Rivington worked for a nonprofit Redd had never heard of that dealt with women's rights and abuse. There was a small photo from the company website attached. Dawson's note said that the two women knew each other and had been briefed on the phone, but for whatever reason, preferred to be interviewed in person.

He heard Kathryn go into their bedroom and close the door, so he shut down the computer and went to talk to her. She was fine with him going. Douglas was going to stay for another day to buy supplies in town and look into going to Europe. She would have some company, and he would be gone only one night. He had not heard from Marta, so he texted her but did not get a response. His phone showed that she had notices silenced. He hoped she was getting a good night's sleep. She should be exhausted by now.

59

So Why Kill Tom?

In the morning Redd left for the airport at 8:00. Marta's phone was still blocking texts. He intended to call her when he got through security, but Berry called him, and the two of them discussed what he had read in the reports the night before. Berry told him that the preliminary reports from Europe so far that day were from small galleries who admitted to having received framed pieces of American and primitive artwork for individuals for a small fee that supplemented their revenues, which were meager for the most part. Pieces came in from time to time and were usually collected within a few days. The last delivery had been about a month ago. None of them had any pieces still waiting to be picked up. The report from the various police reports in the field stated that almost all of the individuals seemed reluctant to talk and gave information haltingly. None of them had addresses for the clients, only phone numbers, which when tried went to dead ends.

"It was all pretty clever, you know," said Berry. "You set up a process that doesn't arouse suspicion, the art exporting, and then begin to send the drugs through a legitimate channel, a legitimate importer, who collects the duty and pays it on to the governments involved, then he ships the artwork to a local shop where a customer who ordered it comes to pick it up. Different drop-off points in different cities, no immediately discernible connection."

"Until someone got in the middle."

"There have been stories in some high-end art magazines about drugs being moved around through the art world in various ways. If I were guessing, based on the timeline of events to date, I'd say one scenario could be that one of the art dealers got suspicious and drilled into one of those metal frames. Suspicion confirmed, he drilled a larger hole in the back to remove the drugs, refilled the frame with an equal weight of something or other, patched the hole with JB Weld, and covered it with some sort of printed label. Then he'd send them on to the customers who had ordered them, in a timely fashion, and split with the goods. It would be a few days to a week at least before the frames started showing up at the final destinations without the drugs in them.

"I'm starting to scare myself," said Berry. "Thinking like a criminal. I could be making a lot more money if I flipped to the dark side."

"Ha! You wouldn't last long," laughed Redd. "Wouldn't the recipients have gone back to the little art dealers where they picked the pieces up?"

"They might have. But I'm guessing by now this has to be a network, so they would report back to someone, and it would become obvious that it was happening all over the place, so they had to go back to the source. The guy in England goes looking for Nathan and calls Tom, and Nathan goes looking for the agent. That's why he went to Florence and wherever. Then he disappears, and Tom goes looking for him and for the product too."

"Killing everyone doesn't get them anything back, though, so why kill Tom?"

"I can't answer that."

"Well, I need to board, so let me know when you can." Redd hung up and boarded. He was the last person on, and he put his phone on airplane mode as soon as he sat down, due to an admonishment from the flight attendant.

60

She Checked Out

There was a slowdown due to air traffic backups into Chicago, so Redd had to hurry from the E gates in terminal 2 to the C gates out in the outer terminal building for United at O'Hare. He boarded as soon as he got to the gate area and texted Kathryn first, who texted back that all was well and wished him a good trip. He then tried to call Marta, but the call went to voicemail. He was beginning to worry. He had stored the hotel phone number, so he called there next and opted for reception on the automatic menu.

When the receptionist picked up, Redd asked her to connect him to Marta's room and gave her the number.

It was quiet for a minute as he heard the receptionist typing on her computer. "I'm sorry, but there's no one in that room. She checked out this morning."

"Are you sure? Where did she go?"

"Well, I'm sure she checked out, but I have no idea where she went."

"Did she ask you to call a taxi or anything?"

"No, but she could have done that herself."

"Of course. Humm, I wonder if she went home. I guess the local taxi service could take her down to Lexington for enough money."

"We occasionally have a taxi take someone to the airports at the Valley up by Weyers Cave or to Charlottesville, so I'm sure she could have got one."

"Okay. Well, thanks."

Redd immediately called Berry and left a message. This worried him. And he couldn't do anything about it for another thirty or more hours. He scrolled through the online yellow page options for taxis on his phone. He didn't recall having had any incidents involving taxis when he was sheriff and was surprised when he thought about it that he was completely unfamiliar with what might be offered. The airplane door had closed, and he needed to turn off his phone. It would have to wait until he was in LA. He just hoped that Marta was safe. He should have tried to hand her off to Berry or a safe house, but the danger seemed to be gone. He just hoped she wasn't going to do something stupid. Like go to Europe to look for Nathan.

61

Gabe Had Some Pills

Redd fell asleep on the flight from Chicago and didn't wake up until they were an hour or so out of LA. He made some notes on what he and Berry had discussed and then wrote down a few questions or points he wanted to clear up with the two women in Los Angeles. He only had the briefest of descriptions of what they did and dates when they would have crossed paths with the dead sister and with Dunbar.

By the time he landed and got to the hotel it was nearly 4:00 local time. He was due to meet the women at 5:00, so he checked in and took a shower and put on a fresh shirt, pressed khakis, and pulled on a light cashmere sweater since the room was cold and the hotel felt damp and cool. It was much warmer than Virginia, but still a cool day in Los Angeles, only in the low 50s.

He went down to the lobby to wait for the two women. He had looked at the small conference room, and it was cold and charmless. So he decided that if he could find a section of the lounge area that would provide some privacy and they could get a glass of wine, that would be preferable. He picked a sofa and chair arrangement at the far end of the area with a low cocktail table in the center. He moved one of the chairs slightly to discourage anyone else from wanting to sit near, and called to a waiter and ordered a sparkling water.

He had texted to both numbers, and a few minutes after 5:00 the two women came in together. He stood and waved, and they came over to the table. After introductions, they all took seats and he called the waiter back for drink orders. The women ordered spritzes, and Redd ordered a small glass of Pinot Noir and some appetizers for the three of them.

"I appreciate you taking the time to talk to me," said Redd, "and having to change plans. The other gentleman had to go home for a family health issue. But I just have one question first: why did you want to meet in person and not just talk over the phone?"

"It was me that insisted on that," said Rachel, the blond women's rights advocate. "I got scammed a while back, and I know its nuts, but I have been leery ever since. Besides, they told me the guy was going to be out here anyway checking on Sandy's place up in Sacramento, I think it was, so it was no big deal. I'm sorry you had to make a special trip, but if it's that important to Gabe, he can pay for the damn expense of it."

"Okay, I understand, I just wanted to clear it up. Just so you're comfortable, I used to be the sheriff in a county in Virginia and now do special cases for the FBI. This is a bit of a side favor for an attorney I know in Virginia, and the circumstances are unusual. Do you know what this is about?"

The other woman, Deborah, the actress, spoke. "We were told that Gabe is being charged with Sandy's murder, but that a body hasn't been found."

"That's essentially it. Gabe, Mr. Dunbar, insists on his innocence, and there was something on social media, which I understand came from one or both of you, if that's right, about his relationship with family and the younger sister?"

"Damn right," said Rachel. "He's the reason Julia is dead, the reason her mom and dad are dead."

"So, tell me why you think this?" said Redd.

"Think it hell—this isn't a conjecture. We know it. He roofied Julie in college, and he and a couple of other guys raped her."

Deborah nodded in agreement.

"Why wasn't he charged at the time?"

"Hah, what kind of sheriff were you? You know why he wasn't charged. The guys said it was consensual. Have you ever heard of a roofie case leading to a rape charge? Never. It's why I work for women's rights."

"Alrighty, just tell me what you know. I never encountered anything like this when I was sheriff. Rapes, yes, but not roofie related, so I have never been involved in an investigation. Can we just stick to this situation and start by you telling me how you knew everyone, when and where, and then what happened."

Deborah spoke. "Rachel, don't jump on this guy, okay? Let's just tell him what he needs to know. Mr. Herring, Deborah and I were friends with Julia back when we were at UVA. And we knew her sister, Sandy."

"Okay, and how long did you know these various people?"

"We met Julia when we were in junior year, took many of the same classes and started to hang out together. That's how we met Sandy, Julia's sister, who was sort of friends with Celia. And then we met Gabe, Celia's boyfriend, probably a few months after we started hanging out with Julia. And then at parties."

"Were you close to Celia? What was your relationship with her?"

"I couldn't stand Gabe," said Rachel. "I always thought he was too slick, and I didn't think he treated Celia well. Sandy wasn't really that close to any of us, but she was one of several people who always seem to end up at the same parties, you know. It's all a bit incestuous at times."

"Alright, let me see if I've got this straight. The two of you and Julia are friends. Celia is what, three years older?"

"Yes, about that," said Rachel.

"And you met Celia and her then boyfriend Gabe while they were in grad school and law school and met Sandy around the same time?"

"Yeah, I mean there were a lot more people in the group that we knew. It wasn't that long ago, but those are the ones you're interested in, isn't it?"

"Yes, exactly. Now tell me about this roofie incident and how you came to know about it."

"Okay, but first, we should tell you that Celia and Julia weren't that much alike. I mean they were both beautiful, and guys were after them, but Celia was the outgoing one—I mean, she liked to party. She was super smart and all, but she liked to party big-time, and I know she was a bit wild before she and Gabe got together."

"What about Sandy? Where did she fit in this mix back then?"

"She and Celia knew each other, but I'm not sure how well," said Deborah. "I'm pretty sure Gabe wanted to hook up with Sandy. I'd see them at parties, and he'd have his eye on Sandy until Julia caught him and gave him shit. I never cared for Gabe, either. I mean it seems like everyone is on the make in college, but Gabe was the worst. I'm certain he cheated on Celia when they were engaged."

"Unfortunately we never actually caught him at anything," said Rachel.

"Don't be silly. You know he screwed that one girl—what was her name? Louisa something? Anyway, you're right. That's not what we're here to talk about."

Redd felt like he needed to get the conversation back under control. "Yes, let's stick to what you know for certain, and more about the roofie incident that you saw that caused all the problems and Julia's death."

"Yeah, you're right," said Rachel. "So, the night it happened there was a party, in our senior year, almost graduation time, at a house out from town a ways. Some business school guy with lots of inherited money had this amazing house—I mean for anyone, not just a student—and there were maybe a hundred people there. I don't think Celia was there that night—no, I'm sure she wasn't—she had the flu or something, or this would never have happened. So, Julia and the two of us went on our own. I don't remember who invited us—doesn't matter. So, Gabe was there, but I'm not sure Sandy was, either. I don't recall seeing her there. Yeah, that's right."

Deborah picked up the story. "At some point Julia disappeared. I know she had had a few more drinks than normal, or they were mixed stronger, the guys would do that, and she disappeared for a while. At one point Gabe and some of the guys also disappeared upstairs somewhere. So what had happened was that Gabe had roofied her, and he and a couple of his buddies raped her."

"How do you know it was Gabe?" asked Redd.

Deborah looked at Rachel who replied, "We were all pretty drunk, and one of the guys let slip that Gabe had some pills and they got in someone's drink. He never said who's drink, and we didn't think that much about it until after."

"Well, later he kind of bragged about it."

"Yeah, he did," added Rachel. "Like it was a cool, manly thing to do. Sick."

"Okay. Julia disappears, you two are still there, what happened next?" asked Redd.

"Well, it got kind of late, and we needed to get back to the dorm, and we needed to find Julia. She had passed out from the roofie, so we finally got someone to help us get her in a taxi and back to the dorm. It wasn't until the next morning that Julia woke up and was sore and realized that she had been raped while she was passed out."

"What did she or any of you do?"

"We wanted her to report it, but she was too ashamed. We actually begged her to, but she finally got angry with us and wouldn't speak to us for a bit. But you could tell she was having a bad time. She went into depression and actually dropped out of school just before graduation. It was terrible," said Deborah.

"That's a terrible story," said Redd. "I'm sorry to hear that it happened. What eventually happened with her then? Did she ever report it or seek counseling, do you know?"

"We don't know, but we tried to stay in touch," answered Rachel. "We would hear stuff from time to time, but after graduation we all went different directions. I got married, which didn't suit me, so I divorced him, and Deborah and I reconnected out here. One of our Facebook friends kept closer touch with the family—I think she knew Julia and Sandy's mom and dad and told us Julia had started some sort of drug thing to help with the depression, but it didn't help and she eventually took an overdose."

"So, it was not recreational drugs?"

"No, not that I know of," said Rachel. "Where did you hear that?"

"It was on social media according to one of the background reports they gave me. Okay, this helps."

"The important thing, and the absolutely unforgivable, tragic thing, is that Gabe and his roofie pill and his buddies as good as killed her that night. And eventually her parents too," said Deborah.

"What do you mean? About the parents?" asked Redd.

Deborah replied, "They were killed in a car crash about two years, maybe a little less, after Julia died. They hit a truck.

But I'm convinced they did it on purpose. They couldn't stand the loss of their Julia."

"That's a strong accusation," said Redd. "What evidence do you have?"

"I can't prove it, but our friend on Facebook said they were not doing well and were very depressed. They had put a lot of faith in Julia, had really helped her along, since she wasn't as outgoing as Sandy, I guess, and this really destroyed them."

"I'd be careful making those kinds of statements, if I can give you some advice," warned Redd. "I was thinking of asking for the name of your Facebook friend, but I'll leave that be for now. The law firm can decide. Do you happen to know the names of the other guys who were allegedly involved in this attack on Julia?"

The two women looked at each other. "I know the names of some of the people who were at the party," said Rachel, "but I don't know who went in the room and raped Julia, no. You should ask Gabe that. His ass is the one on the line right now."

"I will. I'll get the law firm to work on that to see what it turns up. I have one more question, and then I'll let you go, or I'd be happy to buy you dinner here or somewhere, if you'd like."

"We both have places to be," said Rachel, "but thanks anyway. What was your question?"

"What do you think might have happened in Virginia at Gabe's house? He admits to having sex with Sandy, and there are things that would indicate that is true, and then she is gone when he wakes up, supposedly. How violent, if at all, is or was this guy? Is he capable of murder? And why would he kill her?"

"That's just it," replied Deborah. "Why would he? He'd wanted to screw her for ages, gets the chance, hopes for more. No, I think she set him up."

"So, one more question, something I should have asked. Where was Sandy during all this time that Julia was suffering and depressed and after she died? Did she ever try to help her sister or her parents? I meant to ask that earlier."

"I don't know. She was always a lot colder and less emotional in a way. Not unkind to Julia, but I think maybe she resented her a little, didn't you, Rachel? Maybe because the parents had put so much effort into Julia, more than into Sandy?"

"That's probably true. But it did get to her, and she was concerned when things got really bad, and I think that's part of what broke up her marriage, is what I heard from friends and on Facebook and her tweets sometimes."

"Well, that helps," said Redd. "You have both been very generous with your time, and I appreciate your help. If you think of anything else you believe might help, you have the number for the partner at the law firm, I believe."

"Yes, and I apologize for the comments about your sheriff abilities," said Rachel. "I get a sense you are good at what you do."

Redd chuckled. "I try to be. I hope you both have a good evening."

They shook hands with him and left. Redd called for the bill, signed it, and went to his room. The conversation had ruined his appetite in many ways. It was now after 6:30 in LA which meant it was 9:30 in Virginia. He called Kathryn and told her briefly about the conversation and about Marta leaving the hotel and not answering her phone. Kathryn told him everything was fine there. She and Douglas had had a relaxing evening talking about pleasant parts of their childhood. He wished her good night and clicked off. He tried to call Berry but didn't get an answer and left an updated message about Marta.

The hotel had a restaurant with a decent reputation, but he didn't feel up to a full meal. He ordered a large Greek salad from room service and took the next hour to clean up his notes and eat the salad. He went to bed by 8:30 local time, 11:30 in Virginia.

62

Impeding an Investigation

Redd was awake by 4:30 a.m. A few moments after he woke up his phone buzzed with a message from Berry: "Tried calling M Miller, checked CC, she charged ticket to Amsterdam, left yesterday. Has arrived by now, not answering texts, you need to go find her."

Crap, crap, crap, thought Redd. *I should have handed her over to Berry or locked her in a room somewhere. She's going to get herself killed.* He called Berry.

"Son of a bitch," said Redd when Berry answered.

"Yeah. We should have put her in a safe house."

"Well, send someone else to find her. She nearly already got herself and Kathryn killed."

"That wasn't exactly her fault," said Berry.

"I know, I know, but the last thing she needs to be doing right now is chasing after that son. I'm surprised she went to look for him. From what she told me, she was ready to divorce her husband and was disappointed in the son and hadn't spent much time around him. That doesn't mean she wants him dead, but still, she has to know the risks. I mean, they came after her here. And they've killed both her husband

and probably the agent. Who knows what they'll do to her if they catch her."

"You worked with her. She'd be more likely to listen to you, wouldn't she?" asked Berry. "Or you could just cuff her and bring her home. Impeding an investigation, whatever."

"You've been reading your own bulletins and memos too often. See what your Interpol guys can find. I'm in LA and won't be back until this afternoon, and I have to report to the attorneys in Charlottesville. This one is a situation with a messy past, apparently. I told you the basics earlier."

"This is the missing woman and the local investment guy— or attorney—who's accused of murder? But no body?"

"Yeah, that one. It turns out this guy, Dunbar, the suspect, may have roofied the younger sister of the woman who's missing. The sister took an overdose after suffering depression from the incident and died, and then the parents may have killed themselves in a car accident shortly thereafter. So some former classmates think the missing woman might have set this up in retribution."

"That's a bit over the top. It exposes her to lawsuits and criminal charges of all sorts."

"I know, and from what I've heard about her, I don't think she's stupid, so I don't know what the plan is. We have to find her first. *They* have to find her first. Unless he really did kill her."

"I'll get back to you. I'll see what Interpol can do. We could have had them intercept Marta if we had known she was on the plane. Let me see what I can do."

63

Patient Privacy Rule

Redd called Lawrence and gave him a summary of what he had found.

"I spoke with him earlier about rumors of rape on Facebook. He denied it. Said it was consensual. How do you think we proceed? I'll ask him again and tell him we have corroboration."

"Is he really so obtuse, if this did happen, to not have some suspicion of the sister, Sandy? And a little depraved to want to have sex with her? I mean, what sort of guy is he?"

"I don't know him that well. Just another young lawyer, eager to make a name for himself. Aggressive at his firm. Smart. I don't know, I suppose guys fantasize about sisters at times. Who knows, we'd need to talk to a therapist or someone about stuff like that. But let's see what he says now. Did the two women know the names of the other participants? I'll call them."

"No, you'd have to go back and do some work on who attended the party and get names from people who were there and might know more. The women were downstairs away from whatever took place and found out the next morning when Julia woke and told them. You know what to do. Get your research guy to get on the internet and find who was at the party and someone out there will eventually tell you the truth. I'm guessing what the women said was true, and the outcome supports that thesis. I don't know if she had a therapist, or if you could even get medical or other records. The patient privacy rule goes out fifty years after death doesn't it?"

"Generally, unless there's been a crime related to death, or you were a paid carer, or a close family member. Unfortunately, that family member is now missing. Let me think about that. A judge might give us an opening based on a probable crime, and we could, maybe, establish a link. It's a stretch, but if we think the patient information is that valuable, which I think it would be here, then maybe."

"I don't know the law, but it makes sense. I need to go. Let me know what you find out."

Lawrence's response surprised Redd a bit. "It really is a failure of the system that women feel ashamed or that it's useless to report such incidents. I know we go on proof, but this is such abuse. Well, let me talk to Dunbar and the researcher and my partners about the approach we just discussed, and I'll get back to you. Send me your charges and mileage, and we need to figure out your fee."

"Okay. Let me know what you find out."

64

Unsettled

Redd showered and dressed and went down to the restaurant and had a forgettable breakfast with undercooked potatoes and overcooked eggs and coffee that was just passable. He went back to the room and brushed his teeth and put his toilet kit into his small carry-on bag and got the hotel shuttle back to the terminal. The whole experience had left him unsettled. He thought about Dunbar, a young attorney who was either very successful early on, based on where he lived, or he had some family money. Dunbar's wife, Celia, who also had looked like she came from money, something about her confidence even in a stressful situation. She had asked him to leave and was used to getting her way. He supposed they'd checked her alibi for the time Sandy went missing. He'd remind Lawrence. It was a long shot.

Of more immediate concern for now was Marta. It looked like she had taken advantage of his absence to get out of the country to go look for her son. Why hadn't she gone to greater efforts to get him to help her? Probably because she knew he would discourage her from going at all. But she must know the danger. After all, Tom was dead, two men had shot their way into her house, one had tried to break into her hotel room, they had burned part of her son's shop, attacked and killed a sheriff's deputy, and been stopped only by being killed themselves. And the agent was missing, and it looked like so were a lot of illegal drugs. How much stronger could the warning be? Was a mother's love that strong, or was something else going on? He thought back to their conversations after the attacks, and how she had described growing to hate her husband and being concerned more about money going forward than about his safety.

He had meant to ask Berry to check on her departure and arrival times with customs but had forgotten. He assumed Berry would do that on his own. Berry said they had gotten the information from monitoring the credit card. But just in case, he texted Berry and asked him to run a check on her passport and entries and exits. He wondered if she had gone back to the house with the deputy a couple of days before to get it. Most likely.

He boarded the plane and tried to put both Dunbar and Marta Miller out of his mind by watching a classic Hitchcock movie on the seatback screen in first class on the way to Chicago.

65

Russian Stacking Dolls

There were no messages for him when he reached Chicago. He texted Kathryn and said he should be home by dinnertime and they could go into town if she wished, or he could meet her in Charlottesville after he landed and they could have an early dinner there. She texted back to just come home and she would fix something. Douglas had left to go back to Monterey that morning.

When he landed in Charlottesville and turned off airplane mode there was a text from Berry to call him immediately.

"What's up?" Redd asked.

"What did Miller tell you about her travels this past year?"

"I don't recall precisely. She mentioned the cruise from England to Iceland or somewhere back in the summer, I think it was. That was the only one out of the country I remember. She said she was gone a lot, but I got the sense it was to Florida with girlfriends. Why?"

"Well, she's been lying. She's been in Europe at least three times since June."

"She did mention some trips with Tom to France and Rome,

but I didn't get a timeline. I did think they were maybe earlier, though."

"They weren't to Paris or Rome. One was to London back in July, right after the trip she told you about with her husband. One was to London the end of May, then back from Iceland two weeks later. But the end of July she went to London from Miami, was gone three days total."

"So, she was in Miami after all, but didn't stay there? We might have checked the trip to Miami, but there wasn't any reason to as far as I could tell," said Redd.

"No, it wouldn't have seemed to have mattered. So, the next trip was early September to Amsterdam, again from Miami, then a return from Florence, four days later."

"What the hell? The very places Nathan supposedly went to."

"Yeah, well, that's not all, she was back in Amsterdam for two full days it looks like in early November, and I checked and that would be about the time of the last big shipment of drugs to Rotterdam from Nathan's shop in Charlottesville."

"What in the heck was she up to? She must have been as much a part of this as Tom and Nathan."

"Or," said Berry, "to be more exact. What if she was the one who was setting it up and not Tom?"

"Then that would mean she must have had Tom killed."

"Might not have planned it, but we have to consider it, and consider her a criminal now and get Interpol looking for both her and Nathan."

"You think they were in it together?"

"Well, think about it. He's missing, and so is she, and they've been to the same places—her first, then him later."

Berry had moved down the hall in the terminal where he could have more privacy. "I need to wrap my head around this. What are you suggesting now?"

"I want to send a team down to go through his apartment and see if anything was missed, then we go through the house down by Lexington and do one more look at the shop. I'll have Interpol take a second look at the agent's office, and I've asked them to try and locate the Russian—Blaskoff, or whatever he's called. It's too coincidental that he disappeared as all this came down. I just wish I knew who stole what and who they stole it from."

"But the video showed Tom meeting with the Russian, and Nathan too, of course."

"Smokescreen, my friend, I'd bet anything. Tom either thought he was in charge, or he didn't have a clue what was happening, and she had the Russian meet him."

"No," said Redd. "He had to be involved. She just outfoxed him. Like she did me."

"Like she did everybody. You thought you were protecting her."

"I've been giving that some thought. Questioning whether I would have handled this in the same manner if she had been fifty-five and plump. Yeah, I wonder about that shootout now, and her gun skills. Crap, she could have gone through stuff at my house while she was there. But she would have already known how the search was going, since she set it up. How clever, jeez. But I think those Albanians were not planned. That's the other side being seriously pissed about losing the drugs, so who knows who sent them. I don't think it would have been the cartel. They wouldn't send Albanians, would they? This is your bailiwick."

"No this has Russian roots, I think. If this was cold war spy days, I'd say it was a double double-cross, and Mrs. Miller's Russian partner was trying to take her out of the picture and keep the whole piece. It's like one of those Russian stacking dolls."

"Well, it's all speculation right now. I need to get home. Let me know if you need me at any of the searches."

Redd clicked off and went out to get his pickup out of the ridiculously high-priced parking lot, then texted Kathryn to let her know he was on his way. He turned the ringer off on the phone and put it in the glove compartment, out of reach.

66

Crazy Women

When he got home, Redd told her just a bit about the California trip but really wanted Kathryn to know what he had just learned about Marta. He would talk to her about the other case tomorrow.

"Geez, it's a good thing she didn't kill us while we were asleep," said Kathryn.

Redd laughed, but the laugh was an uneasy one. Marta had been so convincing as the concerned wife and mother.

"I won't take another case from Berry without it being vetted first. I should have known that missing persons cases are not that simple. They never have been. We still have people we haven't found from a couple of cases ago, as you know, and that one on Hawaii was a real mess."

"Of course I know. What are going to do now?"

"I'm letting Berry take it back." He explained what they had discussed after he landed.

"I hope that's the end of it. It looks like that woman was a lot more dangerous than anyone suspected. I guess her ability to handle a rifle should have told us all something."

"Does that mean I need to watch out for you too?" Redd laughed. "You were a damn good shot as well."

"I'd sleep with one eye open if I were you," she laughed. "Speaking of which—that woman getting in bed with us and pretending to be distraught. I think maybe she was hoping I'd let her get in the middle and she could have her way with you. Or maybe a ménage et trois? I might need to get you analyzed. You seem to attract some crazy women. Not including me in that number, but jeez, it seems there's one in every case you take on."

"Well, let's hope this one is gone," said Redd. "I wonder where she is right now. I wonder what was in Tom's will? I guess she might be a rich woman right now. Douglas didn't find the balances in the accounts, but just the amounts that had come in. I should get him back here to look deeper."

"Well, let's forget about all that for now, have a nice dinner and a normal night for a change. I made a variation on Amatriciana, and I've got a nice bottle of Prisoner from California to serve with it. Fitting, I might say."

During dinner they talked about the old Hitchcock movies and the women in his movies, and how badly he had apparently treated them, but how good the movies were, and the classiness of the actors, dressed in suits and ties for the men and dresses that were likely designer, for the women. Neither one watched many movies these days. After dinner Redd helped clean up and they went to bed early and made love for the first time in almost a week.

67

Where Is the Justice?

The temperature had begun dropping overnight, and it was supposed to get bitterly cold with wind, so Kathryn had directed the two cowboys to move the cows and heifers to pastures where they would have access to barns that would shelter them from the worst of the wind. Cold didn't really affect them all that badly with their winter coats which developed when they were left out in the pastures as it got colder in the autumn. But the wind would make it feel like temperatures well below zero, and Kathryn wanted her cattle protected.

She didn't have to go to school until late morning, so Redd took advantage of the time to give her a better overview of the conversation in California and Sandy's possible motives for revenge.

"Another surprising woman, if she really did that," said Kathryn. "I guess she figured trying to get him for rape at this late date was impossible, and just accusing him of it would not have much more effect than it seems to have with politicians, so it would have been pointless."

"It's extreme and carries great potential personal cost for her, though," said Redd.

"Yes, but a lot of people will see strength and nobility in that."

"Okay," said Redd, "but if he didn't kill her and is convicted and goes to prison, where is the justice in that?"

"Where is the justice in this guy and his buddies raping a woman who they drugged and getting away with it? And worse, a woman who later takes her own life because of it? They should have been charged at the time. So punishment now is appropriate."

"I see your point, have seen it all along, but it's a form of vigilantism, and we can't have that."

"Then the law needs to do a better job, or the justice system anyway. But you know that."

"Yes, but the job right now is to find out if he did or didn't kill her," said Redd. "There are no other fingerprints in that house except his and his wife's and that woman's. She had to have a security clearance for the tech company, so hers are on file. And there was blood upstairs and in the basement drain."

"But he has a pretty weak motive, a supposed blackmail effort of a hundred thousand—unless she threatened to expose him for the rape, but he would just have denied it, so that's out. I think she set him up and will have to be satisfied with what it does for his reputation—unless someone can get the guys who were with him to come forward, or someone feels guilty enough to fess up. And no one is chasing that angle as far as I can tell from what you've told me. It's just those couple of women on social media."

"He'll just keep denying it unless someone comes forward, you're right," said Redd.

"Will his wife divorce him, do you think?" asked Kathryn. "I guess there's no way to know about that."

"No, she's angry, but I'm not sure where the anger is directed right now. We'll have to see how it plays out. What a mess, two women and one guy we can't find. I need another line of work."

Kathryn headed back to the bedroom to change to go to the university, and Redd headed to his office. He had just started his computer when his phone rang, and it was Berry.

"Now what?" said Redd. "Did you find her?"

"No, just listen. She doesn't own the house where you met with her that got shot up."

"Go out. What are you talking about?"

"It was sold and closed on three months ago, and she and Tom rented it back for ninety days."

"Where were the new owners? How did you find them?"

"They showed up while our agents were there this morning. They'd been on a cruise out in the South Pacific and weren't planning to come back until the end of the month, but they saw an old news story somewhere that showed the house, and when they couldn't get Miller or McFerren on the phone, they came back to see what the hell was going on."

"Man, this just gets worse and worse. Did she think we'd never figure it out?"

"I don't suppose she cared. If we had, she'd just say they had rented it back and were moving but hadn't found a place, who knows, but it does look like she or Tom or both were cashing things in. Apparently, the house was in her name. Probably to keep it out of the hands of some of Tom's creditors or people he cheated over the years."

"What did it sell for?"

"A million-four, which is cheap for that house, but it's so isolated."

"So have your agents found anything yet?"

"No, not yet. Surprisingly few women's clothes, they reported, desk drawers mostly empty, no computer, of course, normal kitchen stuff, normal bedding, no hidden safe, no guns given that she was such a good shot. There must be another house or apartment we don't know about somewhere else. But no record of that found so far."

"Well," said Redd, "the surprises just keep coming. Call me when you learn something else."

68

Lack of a Body

Kathryn poked her head in to say goodbye while Redd was on the call. What a mess, he thought, what a mess. He once again kicked himself for not looking deeper before and while he was working with her, but that was spilt milk.

A few minutes later Lawrence called him. "I just wanted to update you on my conversation with Dunbar this morning. How are things going on your end?"

"Ha, other than being completely outfoxed at every junction by my client—no, I won't call her a client any longer, my project assigned by the FBI—everything is fine. How did it go this morning?"

"He still says sex with the sister was consensual and doesn't want us to look for anyone else who was at the party or anyone who might have taken part. I told him that this is his best defense, that we have to show why Sandy might have wanted to take revenge. But he says he wants to stick with her having bad information, and depend on lack of motive on his part, and lack of a body, and go with that."

"How do you think the prosecution is going to handle it? I

don't think I've had a case with no body before. What are his chances of beating the charge?"

"I have no idea. I mean we will focus on the lack of a body, but the prosecution will certainly want to use the rape allegations in their favor, as a reason for him to get rid of her to keep that quiet. I don't know what the judge will allow, since this is just hearsay and innuendo. But I can think of ways they can get it into the trial through a sort of back door by going back and examining his history with her from the college days, and with the sister and her friends. We will have character witnesses to bolster our case, but they may have something that goes the other way. I just don't know. This is new legal ground for me."

"So, neither of us is having a good day."

"You could say that."

"Something that has been in the back of my mind, if he didn't kill her and dispose of her body, is how did she get out of town? Which I really think happened. I don't think he killed her. Otherwise, why leave any bloody cloth around or the towel or whatever, or leave blood in the drain. He's an attorney, he must know it would be found."

"But we checked all the flights out that day and the next, and her name wasn't on any of the manifests."

"She must have had an accomplice or a friend or something. I think he had to rush to clean up when his wife was coming back two days early, and he only had a couple of hours to make the bed and do the laundry, and he just panicked and didn't get it all done right."

"But why did he drive off to the mountains? He's got to know he can be tracked. And he should at least have left his cell phone at home, if he didn't want anyone to know where he went."

"I don't think there was a dead body in the car. There was no evidence of blood."

"There were hair strands in the back and on the seat."

"They went to dinner. She rode with him."

"Still, I think the cops, or someone, need to go back up in the hills and do some more searching. If they don't find anything, that makes a murder less certain. Doesn't rule it out, but you still don't have a body, and you've tried to find one, and that might help with a jury. I mean this could be nothing more than him trying to hide evidence of that night's screw from the wife.

"If I give you the information we have from the cops, from his phone for that day, could I get you to go up there and look around? I mean you know the area better than anyone. Didn't you have a case in that part of the mountain a while back, or was that further north?"

"Both," said Redd. "There was an accident going south, and the other was more north. Yeah, I'll do it. Can you send me the GPS locator info or however it's been recorded, and I'll go look. The snow melted a lot before this last cold snap."

"I think what you want are the major stopping points. He was at one of the lookouts for the longest. I'll send you the info on that."

"Alright, I'll head up this afternoon," said Redd.

"Good luck."

69

Evidence

Redd was due to go to court in about a week to provide evidence in a case from the previous year. But he had some free time, so he decided that as soon as he got the coordinates for the lookout up on the parkway, he would head up and look around.

In order not to step on any toes, he put in a call to the Charlottesville police and asked for Lieutenant Franklin, who was heading up the investigation. She had also taken over the investigation into the burning of the shop and had spoken to Redd after the sniffer dogs were in.

"Good morning, Lieutenant. This is Redd Herring again. How are things with you?"

"Not bad. Which missing person are you calling about, the woman or the guys?" she laughed.

"Ha, that seems to be my role in life these days. I think you know I have been doing some work for Lawrence Luther on the Dunbar case? We talked about that?"

"Yes. What can I do for you?"

"I talked to Lawrence a bit ago, and he wanted to know if I'd go up on the mountain and sniff around and see if I could locate anything near that lookout where Dunbar's vehicle was shown as being parked for a while the day Sandy Wellsley disappeared. Is that okay with you? I don't want to infringe on your territory or mess up anything."

"If it was anyone else," said Franklin, "I wouldn't want them messing around. Go ahead. The snow might have melted enough to see ground disturbance or whatever by now. If there's a body, it's been frozen, so I don't know what state one would be in. We couldn't find anything when I sent two officers up before, and they looked a good distance down a couple of trails that go off from that lookout. I'd send someone along to look with you, but I'm short on people today. You know what you're doing. Give me a report on where you look."

"I will. Have a good day."

Redd put on high-top hiking boots since the trails up there were steep in places and there could still be some snow and ice. He planned to scan the sides of the trail.

The coordinates for the lookout came in as a text a few minutes later, and he left for the mountain. It took him almost forty-five minutes to get to the lookout. The sun was shining, and the ground was frozen, but most of the snow was gone. It had been only a few inches deep, but that was enough to hide a partially buried body or some belongings.

There were four trails going off from that lookout, two on each side of the road. He was looking to the east, down into a valley with steep sides. It was shaped like a bowl with ridges. The little information billboard said that settlers had lived there and grown corn and other grains. It seemed like a very unproductive place to farm.

Across the road there was a flat grassy area to the west, and one trail led down the slope a bit to connect with the Appalachian trail that went from Maine to Georgia. He doubted if Dunbar would have chosen that one. Even in winter there might be hikers. The other trail on the west side led eventually down to the valley below and also intersected the Appalachian but curved around to follow a small stream that fed into a feeder stream to the South River, down near the base of the mountain. Redd didn't think Dunbar would have used it either. He would have been in a rush and would have wanted to get down the trail somewhere and back as quickly as possible.

The two trails that led off to the east were at opposite ends of the parking area. The one furthest south led south and then a bit back southeast to work its way around a peak and then off to the southeast and back east eventually. Redd had hiked it once down to some pools and several small waterfalls that ran in the spring or during wet weather. He thought that trail would not have been a bad choice because no one would hike to those pools in winter, but it ran uphill initially before descending and a man in a hurry carrying a body or some baggage might be tempted to take a track going downhill. So he chose the one nearest the signboard first.

The trail was icy and uneven, and the danger of turning an ankle was even greater than under normal conditions. The first few hundred yards of the trail had very little undergrowth and there would not have been a good place to hide a body. But as the trail descended there were more entangled wild berry vines and other low-growing trees and shrubs. Here and there a wild rhododendron and some holly trees and small shrubs.

He couldn't see where any underbrush had been disturbed anywhere on either side of the trail, and trying to walk in the forest on either side would have been almost impossible due to the number of low-growing bushes and the entangled dormant branches. It seemed obvious that if anything had been hidden, it would have to have been carried in directly from the trail, or he would have had to climb in on his hands and knees. The reports of his appearance that day did not say anything about that degree of dirt on his pants. Redd kept looking for a space that was more accessible. The sun had passed from directly to the south and was slanting through the tree branches, making a dancing pattern on the patches of snow that still lay on the ground.

Redd had gone close to a quarter of a mile now and had seen nothing so far that looked like a hiding place. He decided to turn and head back and see if he could spot something from a different angle. A hundred feet along he could see where a person could slip under some branches of a young oak tree, and there were clumps of hollies here and there. He bent down and moved into the forest about thirty feet and looked around. There were piles of leaves on the ground, and there were areas of disturbance where squirrels, most likely, had churned them up in search of buried nuts. That kind of activity would make it difficult to find any attempt by a human to hide something.

He was about to turn back when he thought he spotted a flash of light, some reflection from something shiny near a holly bush off to his right, a place where a ray of light had filtered through the overstory of the forest. He pushed aside several branches and reached around behind the holly and brushed aside some frozen leaves and spotted the end of a metal luggage tag that was given by the airlines to their frequent fliers. If he had not been looking in that direction at that moment, he would have missed it. It was attached to a black roller bag handle.

Rather than disturb the bag, and hoping to preserve any evidence that might remain in these conditions, he marked the spot by tying his handkerchief to a branch, took a GPS reading, and scuffed up leaves into the area. He hadn't thought to bring a spray can of paint with him. There was no signal, but he had one further up the trail, so he moved uphill until he had a signal, then called Franklin and told her what he had found. He would wait for her and her people where he was. He also called Lawrence and told him what he had found.

70

Power of the Internet

The local TV station had got wind of the developments in the Dunbar case, which had already attracted attention due to his good looks and his job as an attorney. The public liked to see lawyers in trouble, like the famous case in South Carolina where the lawyer shot his wife and son in an attempt to distract from his multi-million-dollar financial crimes. And if the lawyer and his wife were good looking and rich, or at least lived that way, like Gabe and Celia, it was even a better story. A reporter had been following the rape allegations about the sister which had surfaced on Facebook and other social media platforms and was speculating that Dunbar had possibly raped Sandy Wellsley and killed her and hidden her body. He would have gotten away with it if his wife hadn't come home unexpectedly and found the blood. When the story broke that the police had found her luggage hidden in the mountains near where Dunbar's SUV had been parked for over half an hour on the day his wife discovered the blood, reporters from all of the networks descended on the Dunbar house to try to interview Celia Dunbar. Local police had to set up a cordon to keep them away.

It was also reported that Herring, who was already famous for his involvement in several other high-profile cases, had been the one to find the luggage. Social media began to link this case to the gun battle over in the valley and speculated about links between Marta Miller, whose name was well known now as one of the women who had shot a Russian, and the missing woman, in spite of the fact that the only link in any of it was Herring as the investigator. It was proof of the power of the internet to corrupt the truth.

Kathryn was approached at the university, but called the campus police who escorted the reporters off of the grounds and set up security by her office.

Dunbar admitted to the police that he had taken the luggage to the mountains to hide it from his wife. When asked why he didn't just put it in the attic or take it to the office, he said he didn't want to arouse suspicion at the office, and he was just trying to get it out of the house so that he could return it to Sandy when he could get in touch with her. He still maintained that he had not killed her and had no idea where she was. He had panicked, driven by not knowing where she was or why she had gone off like that, and by trying to hide her presence from his wife. And he still denied the roofie incident with her sister.

The chief of police decided that this new evidence and Dunbar's lying increased his flight risk, so asked the judge to rescind bail, but the judge denied the request, and Dunbar was ordered not to leave the county. His passport had already been surrendered. He had been terminated by the law firm and would face disbarment because of lying to the police and hiding evidence of a potential crime.

71

Samantha Tennysen

In Costa Rica, there is a newer airport at Guanacaste called Liberia with flights every day on United, American, and Delta from the US. Nosara is a settlement near there, and you can rent a simple but comfortable one-bedroom cottage with a great view near the water for as little as a hundred dollars per night.

In one of those cottages, Samantha Tennysen, who her friends called Sandy, checked her computer daily for news from the States. She had hated being called Sammy as a kid, so started introducing herself as Sandy, and it stuck. No one but TSA these days and the former liquor store clerks when she was old enough to drink ever looked at your ID and cared about your given name anyway. And Tennysen had been her last name before she married, and she went back to it after the divorce—another thing most people didn't know.

She had been astounded when the local news first reported that Dunbar's wife had returned home much earlier than planned and called the police when she found the blood in the basement. She had not expected that to happen. Her plan had been to wait another day and report a disturbance from a burner phone, something serious enough to get the police in the house. Celia had done her *job for her, and removed the one area of greatest personal risk that she could see, being sued by Dunbar on some grounds.*

She was surprised how quickly the police jumped on the idea of murder. She was just planning to ruin his marriage and do as much damage to his career as she could for a small measure of retribution for his rape of her sister. That had all happened, but she still felt empty. She had decided to have sex with him to leave the stained towel and to keep him from being suspicious of her even being there. She knew he had had the hots for her from college days, and if he had been a nicer person, she might have been interested. She was always wilder and more adventurous than poor Julia.

She had a pretty good idea who the other three guys were who had raped Julia. She wondered if any of them were following what was happening with Dunbar. They probably would adopt the same attitude as Dunbar and refuse to admit to what they had done. She would wait until this case died down and decide when to go back to the US and who to target next.

72

Aleksei and Miller

Two days after Redd had found the hidden luggage, and written up a short report for the police records, and met with Lawrence without Dunbar there, he got a call just after 7:00 a.m. from Berry.

"So, you saved the day again, I see."

"I didn't save anything," said Redd. "This just added to the confusion. I think the guy is probably a slug, the women in LA are most likely right about him drugging the sister, and he deserves punishment for that, but I don't think he killed the missing woman. I think he is telling the truth about panicking. He's not a brave person."

"Are you done with it now?"

"I hope so. The prosecuting attorney is trying to make a name for himself, so he will push as far as he can and blame someone else if he has to go with reduced charges. I really don't want to have any further involvement. Why did you call? Not to discuss this, I'm sure."

"You're right about that. Do you have a few minutes? I have an interesting tale and some work for you."

"Crap. Can I listen to the tale and skip the work?"

"You can, but I hope you won't. Here's the deal. As you know, half of the raids, arrests, what have you, in the drug busting business are due to informants and tips. So, on our end, we've managed to assemble a little bit of helpful information on the case with McFerren and Miller, but the real story has been provided by the Brits and Interpol.

"So, the man who met with Nathan, and then with Tom, Blaskoff who sometimes calls himself Baskin, is the person who is with Miller now, we are almost positive. His real name is Aleksei Federov, and his grandmother was English, English upper class. She was, or is, if she's still alive, quite beautiful and incredibly intelligent. She went to Cambridge, where she studied the classics sometime after it was no longer fashionable, with an emphasis on languages. She was fluent in Russian, French, German, and Italian, in addition to English, of course.

"In her twenties she became enamored of Marxism and the Soviet Union and married a Russian diplomat. The thought is that she was probably a spy, maybe a double agent of some sort, but at any rate, she was seen around Europe and was untouchable. Apparently, she really did believe in communism or at least had hopes for it. But people who knew her a long time ago, say it was greatly a reaction to what she felt were the evils of capitalism and the money her family had accumulated.

"At any rate, Blaskoff, Aleksei, whichever we want to call him, grew up in a privileged position in the old Soviet Union and inherited his mother's ability with languages. He is apparently quite cultured, loves opera and the theater, and is charming and loves women. Not to marry, but as girlfriends. Miller would have been to his taste. More to the point, he held positions in the KGB or its equivalent, but in recent years has pursued business opportunities. Unfortunately for him, he has either not had the right connections, or just hasn't been very good at it. So, he turned to crime.

"For a while he worked with an arms dealer, Rostov, probably supplying weapons to various African states, but the Wagner Group took over most of that, and he became associated with a smaller-time guy who had contacts in Haiti. As you know, Haiti is practically lawless in good times and for quite a while has been anarchic. It was always an easy transshipment point for drugs from South America. The guy he was working with was smuggling drugs into Europe, but Interpol took down his operation in Marseille about six months ago. He is thought to have been looking for another route into France and the continent. And that's where McFerren and the connection come in."

Redd spoke up. "If all this was known about the guy, why didn't someone arrest him?"

"Good question. Apparently, this is the first time all the pieces have come together. And this is fairly new. The concentration in the past was on the arms dealer and the Marseilles connection. Aleksei's name never came up with that, and no one really cared about the weapons going to Haiti."

"Alright," said Redd, "that's a lot of background, but what does that have to do with you and me? It seems to be that the biggest piece of this puzzle is still missing. Who was receiving the drugs in Amsterdam or in all the cities they were going to? And if this guy Aleksei and his new girlfriend Miller decided to hijack them, how do they sell them without getting killed?"

"I'm getting there. This morning the police in Rotterdam pulled two bodies from a canal not far from the warehouse. They have identified one of them as the agent who was handling the artwork for the McFerrens. The other the authorities are almost certain is Rostov, the arms dealer."

Redd was quiet for a moment while the pieces began to fall into place. "Aleksei intercepted the drug shipment to Europe, forcing Rostov and the agent to show up to find out what had happened with them, and arranged for both men to be killed."

"That would be the most logical assumption. Rostov went to Europe after his goons, the Albanians, screwed up and got killed in Virginia. Now, Aleksei will be able to take over the network in Europe."

"Where do you think the drugs are?" asked Redd.

"Doesn't matter. In the pipeline, or he's pulled them out and will start up anew. It's having control of them that matters."

"I can see that. Where are he and Miller now? And where the hell is Nathan—do you think he's dead too?"

"We have no idea where Nathan is. We haven't found a body, but that doesn't mean they didn't kill him and dump him or chop him up and feed him to the fish."

"I don't see anything you need me for right now, so why this call?" asked Redd. "It's all interesting, but I'd say your friends in Europe are doing all they can do."

"Ah, well, in your role as my assistant you are also a Federal Marshall, and tomorrow morning the Czech police along with Interpol are going to raid an apartment in Prague where they are almost certain Aleksei and Miller are staying. Aleksei used to have these bolt holes or safe houses around the continent, and Interpol sent someone around to keep watch, and several people have been seen coming and going. They hope to seize the two of them and maybe the drug stash. I need you to go and help bring Miller back to the States to stand trial here."

"You don't need me for this. You must have a dozen people who could bring her back. Have you noticed me speaking Czech recently?"

"You don't need to speak Czech. Everyone you will work with speaks English. You are the best person to be on the team because you know her. Maybe you can learn where Nathan is, and we can pick him up too."

"Wendell, did you get enough sleep last night? Or the last week? She ran circles around us while she was here and had us looking for Nathan. She's not going to lead us to him."

"That's where you're wrong. If she thinks Aleksei or someone might have him killed, she might well tell you now, because she knows you, and has a sort of relationship with you. The game has changed. A bunch of people are dead, and she's with an experienced ex-KGB guy. She doesn't have many options available to save her son's neck now."

"I don't agree, but I don't have anything else going on right now. I take it you want me to go soon. When is this raid?"

"Tomorrow is what they hope for, could be the next day. I have you tentatively booked for a 2:15 flight out of Charlottesville this afternoon to Dulles and then to Prague through Frankfurt. I booked a hotel for two nights in the center of town and you will be met at the airport and expedited through customs. Dress warmly—it's real winter there. You'll be met by two of our other agents, one woman and one guy. They have all the paperwork for the extradition. The local government doesn't want to deal with her or Aleksei. Any more questions you can give me a call."

Redd hung up and went in to tell Kathryn what Berry wanted and why. He didn't have time to go into the background.

"Prague, huh, one of my favorite cities in Europe. So beautiful. Have you been there?"

"No, well, yes, but only for a day or so on a tour with a teacher group. I always wanted to go back but never did. I don't see this as a major cultural experience."

"It's become a bit of a party city now with Brits flying over for the weekend to get drunk and to get laid. Prostitution is legal I guess there. There are some magnificent buildings and cathedrals, as I'm sure you know. If you didn't have to bring your sniper girlfriend back so soon, I'd come over with you, and we could go visit some stuff."

"I really think this is unnecessary on my part. She's not going to tell me anything she doesn't want to. I'll be surprised if she survives the raid," said Redd.

"Well, you agreed to go. Who knows, maybe something will come of it. What time do you leave?"

"Two this afternoon, I think. I'll check, the booking was being emailed. I'll need to get my passport."

Kathryn gave him a quick peck on the cheek and told him she'd see him in a couple of days.

73

Well, Crap

Redd arrived in Prague the following day at close to noon, after a delayed flight from Frankfurt. He was met as he had been told by a Czech policewoman who spoke excellent English and whisked him through the customs and immigration process. She asked him if he had brought a weapon, and he told her no. She told him that nothing had taken place so far, and he would have an update from an Interpol representative at the hotel.

Because it was offseason, he had been booked, along with the rest of the team, into the Grand Mark Prague which was on the right bank of the river. The safe house where Aleksei and Miller were supposedly hiding out was across the river in Old Town, Mala Strana, with its crooked narrow streets at the foot of the hill on which stood the castle and grand cathedral. Most of the buildings on that side of the river were old. The newer construction was mostly on the south, further back from the river itself.

Redd checked in and, after taking a shower, was met in another suite of rooms by four other people. There were two from the US, a clean-cut young man named Howard Storm who was dressed casually for the meeting, and the female agent who would be with Miller, Clara Prost. Both were polite but reserved. Redd couldn't tell if they resented his presence or not.

The other two were an Interpol detective who would help to lead what they called the incursion into the building and another man equivalent to a local police officer. Redd would wait until they had secured the site, as well as the two individuals they believed to be in the basement-level apartment, before arriving at the site. He would stay a block away with other members of the team. They wanted this to be as discreet and low-level as possible.

After the meeting, Redd took a short nap, and then walked around the streets, over to the old clock that was such a tourist attraction, and then just wandered. It would have been easy to get lost, but he had his phone with him, and when he was ready to head back to the hotel, he just followed the directions on Google Maps. He remembered when he and his wife used to use a map and had to look for the street names to determine where they were. He knew that they learned the cities better that way. The folding paper maps gave them a better sense of location, the big picture, and not just the street they were on. He supposed he could have picked one up from the front desk and done it again, but he was tired and hadn't thought of it.

He went back to the hotel and had a light dinner and a glass of beer. It was lunchtime in the US, and he was hungry after walking around. He went to his room and tried to read but couldn't focus. He kept thinking about all the ways that the next day or two could go wrong. He finally gave up at midnight local time and called Kathryn, who should be back from school by now.

She was just coming in from checking some heifers, and he told her where he was staying but didn't talk about what they would be doing, as he had been told that cell phones might be monitored. She wished him well, and he went to bed and slept soundly until 6:00 a.m. when his alarm woke him. The raid was supposed to be this morning, and he wanted to be up and ready to leave as soon as he was called.

He did not hear anything until 7:00, when Storm, the agent from the US knocked on his door and told him the raid was off for that day. No reason was given, just that the local officials said the timing was off.

Redd went down to the restaurant and had a breakfast of muesli and fruit and some local pastries and two cups of strong coffee. The weather was cold, but the sun was shining. He went to Storm's room and asked him if there was any reason for him to avoid walking around any particular part of the city. Was he likely to be spotted by Miller? That would alert her immediately that they were on her trail. No one had said anything about it the day before.

The agent said he thought it was highly unlikely. Apparently, Aleksei and Miller had only been seen out one or two evenings and never in the daytime. Even then they had only been spotted because the agent who saw them had once handled an exchange with Aleksei and recognized him. He had aged remarkably well with the help of the surgeon's knife and a few nips and tucks under the chin and around the eyes. He looked much the same as he had twenty years ago as a result. No one was sure of his real age.

Redd decided to go to the Museum of Communism and spent the morning there, tracing the history of the Czech Republic and all of the iterations starting primarily at the turn of the twentieth century, up through the first world war, and then the invasion by Germany at the beginning of World War Two. At the end of that war, under the thumb of the Soviet Union, conditions did not improve remarkably for years, and camps and forced labor continued. It seemed to Redd that the country had suffered in some way or other for most of the century.

After lunch, Redd took a short nap and then walked to the river. There was a cold wind, but he was dressed warmly. He crossed the historic Charles Bridge and climbed the steps to the castle and the cathedral where he could look down over the city spread out across the low hills to the south. The river was icy with mists rising from it. It was not navigable for bigger boats.

It had been a good climb up the steps, and after buying a ticket and going into the cathedral and looking around for fifteen minutes or so, he found a café across the square. On the way back down the hill he stopped for a cup of tea and a sweet pastry. The warmth of the café made him drowsy, and he wanted to get back to the hotel for an update. He paid the bill and was back at the hotel an hour later, at close to four o'clock.

He found the two American agents in the bar having a beer and a sausage snack. They had no update for him, but seemed uneasy. Redd sat with them and ordered a sparkling water. After it came, he asked why they seemed concerned.

Storm looked at Prost and said, "I overheard one of them say they had some doubts about something, but when I asked, he said it was nothing. I don't think it's all going as planned, but I have no idea why. I take it you don't either."

"I am just here, like you two, I guess, to deliver someone back to the States. I have no part in anything else."

"But you know the woman, right? You were working with her in the States before she took off."

"Yes. She approached the FBI to help find her husband and son, and I was assigned the job as part of my special role with Wendell, who you work for, or with, I understand."

"Yes, we got a summary. It sounded like we were all a step behind all of the way."

"Is that what's concerning you now?" asked Redd. "Do you think everyone is still a step behind?"

"I really don't know. I shouldn't have said that. I need to go. Prost?"

He called for the check, and they left. *Strange,* thought Redd. *What had he really overheard?*

He was about to go up to the room when he was approached by the Interpol detective and told they would go in in the morning, probably around 5:00 a.m. He gave Redd a secure phone and told him he would let him know when they had the place secure and tell him when to meet to hand over Miller. The plan was to take her straight to the airport, and she would be held by immigration there until flight time.

Redd was tired from the jet lag and all the walking and standing on concrete and pavement. He fell asleep after dinner but woke up at midnight and could not get back to sleep. The raid was on his mind, and he got up at 4:00 and was dressed and ready to go. He went down to the lobby, but the other agents weren't there, and no one else was around, so he went back to his room to wait.

By 6:00 his phone had not buzzed, and he had checked out and was waiting in the lobby to go to the airport. Something was not right. He wondered if they had postponed the raid again.

At 7:00, the Interpol agent came in the front door and walked over to him. "We missed them. They were not there."

"Well, crap."

"Yes, it's not good. Unfortunately, we didn't know all we should have about the apartment. It was one of his safe houses from a long time ago, and it had another exit through a sub-basement into a building behind and into another street. I think they have been gone for at least two days, given what we could tell. He is very clever. There are programmable lights with varying schedules so it would have seemed like something going on even with the heavy shutters they use here. We will check all of the train stations and the airport, but they could be on another continent by now. I am sorry you had to come all this way for nothing."

"I'm sorry you didn't catch them either. We would like to have her back."

"And we would like to have him in our hands. We continue our search. Have a good trip back. I need to go now."

He shook Redd's hand, and Redd gave him back the secure phone. There was no sign of the other two FBI agents.

Redd went into the breakfast room and called Berry, even though it was the middle of the night back home, and told him what had happened. He had already been briefed by Storm who was with the Interpol and local people. Berry told Redd to use his own computer to pick a flight to get home since his tickets were fully changeable and he would catch up with him when he got back.

Redd ordered a cup of coffee and pulled up flight options. The morning connecting flights had now all left, or didn't allow enough time to make it to the airport. He finally found a flight leaving at 2:00 p.m. that would connect in London and get him back to DC that evening. He booked it and decided to see if his room was still available. He would take a nap for a couple of hours and then go to the airport since he hadn't slept much the night before. They would surely not have started cleaning it yet.

The desk agent was cooperative and pleasant and let him go back to the room, but he had to check back in and would have to pay a late checkout fee. Redd was fine with that.

He took the elevator to the eighth floor and walked down the hall to his room, thinking about the morning, the failed raid, and all that had come before it. Maybe this would be the end of his involvement now. He was not qualified to track international criminals.

He touched his key card to the sensor on the door, and it clicked for him to open it. He pushed down on the handle and stepped in, pulling his roller bag along. He inserted the key in the slot that turned on the electricity in the room as the door sighed shut. He turned at a noise, and Marta Miller was standing on the far side of the bed pointing a pistol at him.

74

Marek Will Kill Me

Miller lowered the gun, "Oh, thank God it's you. I didn't know how I was going to get in touch with you."

"What are you doing here? Give me that gun."

"I'll give it to you. I didn't know you had checked out. I found a maid and gave her a hundred dollars to let me in. I told her I was your girlfriend. Oh God, Redd, they're gonna kill me. You've got to get me out of here."

"Who's going to kill you? They were raiding your hideaway this morning, and I was going to take you back to the States. Where were you? What the hell is going on?"

"I know what you must think, but I was just trying to find Nathan, and I came over and found Aleksei and seduced him and…"

"Just stop. Nothing you are saying makes sense, and I don't think any of it is true. Now give me the gun, and I'm calling Berry…"

She raised the gun again. "Don't, I'm begging you, don't. I'll put the gun down, but you need to hear me out. I promise I'll tell you everything I know, but I really need you to get me out of this town and back to somewhere safe, or Aleksei and Marek will kill me."

"Who the hell is Marek?"

"Marek, the Interpol guy, he's in it with Aleksei. I overheard them talking; he warned Aleksei. They go back a long way."

"Holy crap. How can I believe anything you say? You lied to me about the whole deal, when it was you who set up the meetings in Europe, all those trips you never told me about. And then the deaths of Tom and the agent and you disappearing. I don't trust you as far as I can throw you."

Marta started to cry and lowered the gun and came around the bed and handed it to Redd and then pulled herself close to him and held him while she sobbed. At last, he put his free arm around her, and when she had stopped sobbing, he handed her a clean handkerchief to wipe her face and sat her down on the bed.

"I didn't lie—I really didn't. You have it all wrong. I know it looks like I did, but I can explain it all. But I don't have time right now. They will be looking for me. You can't just take me to the airport with you and catch a plane—someone will be watching, and they will get to me and maybe to you too. I know, I know what they can do."

"So what are you suggesting?—not that I'm going to take you up on it."

"You need to leave and go to the main train station—the one up the hill from here—and book two tickets on the 10:35 to Paris thru Munich. We can make it. It's the last train that will get to Paris today. Quick changes in Munich and Stuttgart. They will be watching you when you leave, in case I'm meeting you here. I stole a maid's outfit. I'll sneak out the service entrance and meet you at the station along the platform for the Munich train at 10:35. You take a taxi. Once you leave the hotel they'll forget about you—until you don't catch the plane—but then it will be too late. They can't be everywhere. I'll see you at the train station. Now go."

Redd looked at Marta and started to resist, but something in her look made him believe her, at least for the moment. He hated to let her out of this sight, but she had come to him, looking for him, so why would she split now? He went down to the front desk, checked out again, and went out and asked for a taxi for the airport. One was hailed, and he got in and told the driver to take him to the train station instead, he would pay him extra. He texted the airline to cancel his flight to DC. Redd had kept the gun that Marta had handed to him and placed it in his backpack. He hoped there were no metal detectors at the train station or he would have a lot of explaining to do. His FBI credentials might not be enough.

It was a quick drive up to the train station, and the line for tickets was short. He asked for two first class tickets for the trains to Paris which came to slightly over $800. He made his way to the main waiting area where the Munich train did not yet show a departure track. There was no sign of Marta yet. He didn't know if she planned to walk, which would take thirty minutes, he guessed, not knowing the city that well yet.

A few minutes later the Munich track came up with a departure in fifteen minutes. It was to the left of the station, and he made his way over to that track and walked down the platform to the first-class cars. He paced back and forth, looking at the time on his phone and the station clock constantly. At five minutes before departure time, she had not yet shown up. At three minutes before departure there were just a few stragglers rushing down the platform to jump on the train, including a woman with a shawl and what appeared to be a slight limp, using a cane and carrying only a small bag. She was the last person he could see about to board the train. She glanced up just before she boarded, and he realized it was Marta. He boarded and went to the seats he had reserved. The car had only a few passengers. In a less than half a minute, Marta, still with the shawl, but walking normally, entered the car, and he stood to let her take the window seat next to him. A moment later the train left the station.

"Where is your luggage—don't you have anything with you?" he asked.

"No. I didn't have time to pack anything, and it would have raised suspicions. I left while Aleksei was asleep and stayed in a real dump of a place for two nights. It was almost one of those rooms-by-the-hour places you read about where people go for sex. Prostitution is legal here, but not brothels, so guys meet the girls and either go back to their own hotel or the girl's place or somewhere like where I was. At least they had a decent shower. But I'll need to buy some clothes when we get to Paris. This is all I have, plus this stolen uniform."

There was no one seated near them, but they spoke softly. "You are on the run, and you worry about clothes," said Redd. "Jesus."

"It's just practical. Otherwise, I'll smell like a street person."

"So, you don't think you were followed?" asked Redd.

"No, I'm pretty sure I wasn't, or they would have nabbed me. I took the tram and was the last person on. I don't think they really expected me to try to get in touch with you. You wouldn't, would you—I mean, turn yourself in to the person who is there to arrest you and take you back to the States?"

"Well, at some point I'm going to need to get in touch with Berry. He didn't want me using my cell phone due to security, and I didn't have time before the train. To be honest, I didn't want to tell him in Prague and have him send the agents that were still there to find me. I hope you aren't planning to screw me over again. I'm sticking my neck way out here."

"I won't, I promise. You are saving my life. I'll behave and do as you say from now on. But I need to catch some sleep. Can I do that for a bit? Will you keep an eye on me?"

"Sure, let me go to the restroom first."

A few minutes later he was back, and Marta was already asleep and slumped over into his seat. He righted her, and she leaned against him and fell back to sleep instantly.

75

I'll Behave, I Promise

The train from Prague to Munich took just under six hours, and there was only a nine-minute connection time between that train and the Munich-to-Stuttgart one, but the train from Munich arrived at the same platform the Stuttgart one was departing from, so they only had to walk a dozen feet or so across to it. This leg of the journey would last only two hours, and then there was an hour and a half connection time in Stuttgart for the train to Paris.

The trains had public Wi-Fi, but Redd didn't want to use it. Cell signals also came and went, but he texted to Kathryn that there had been a change in plans and he would be delayed a day or two returning but that all was well. He texted something similar to Berry.

The train from Munich to Stuttgart was nearly full, which surprised Redd. There was a mix of students, professionals, and older individuals and couples, mothers with babies in strollers and bikers who stored their bicycles in rooms provided at the end of some of the cars specifically for that purpose. Neither the Prague-to-Munich train nor this one was an express, so people were leaving and entering the cars frequently. Redd kept an eye out for anyone who might have shown an interest in him or Marta but saw no one.

In Stuttgart, they went to a café in the station, and Marta had a glass of white wine and wiener schnitzel. Redd had a meal with sausages and sauerkraut and a side of potato salad along with a beer. Portions were generous, and Marta only ate a third of her dinner.

They ordered coffee after the meal, and while they were drinking it, Marta said to Redd, "When we get to Paris, I don't want you to put me in a separate room. I want to be with you. I'll behave, I promise, but I'm afraid to be alone. You can get two beds. I'll pay you back."

Redd smiled. "I suppose we could do that. I don't have handcuffs to cuff you to your bed, so I'll just have to trust you. Can't believe I'm saying that. I should go ahead and book a room. We won't get in until close to eleven tonight. We can't get a flight out until tomorrow morning some time."

"I just need to buy a quick change of clothes and some underwear. I can't wear what I have on much longer. Can we just do that in the morning? I'll be quick. You come with me."

"We need to be as quick as possible. The longer we are in Europe the greater the chance they find you."

"I know that. I'm just asking for an hour. We'll have more waiting time than that."

Redd agreed and looked online for a hotel room with two beds. As much as he preferred local hotels, the best option was a Marriott not far from the train station where they would arrive. They could grab a taxi. He found several flight options, but the sites were slow due to a weak signal in the café, and they had to leave to board the train to Paris before he had time to book flights.

They boarded the train a few minutes later for the four-hour ride to Paris.

76

Withholding Evidence

The first-class compartment for this leg of the trip was nearly empty so far. Redd and Marta had seats near one end. Redd had picked up a bottle of water in the station, and they took advantage of the mostly empty compartment and sat opposite each other across a narrow worktable with fold-down leaves.

When the train had cleared the station and they had watched the other trains moving in and out, they could hear the train clicking over the switch points, finding its way out of the city and into the night. Marta said to Redd, "You know, I really didn't lie to you that much."

Redd laughed. "That's good to know. Unfortunately, it's pretty hard to know which parts are which with you. Good to know there is some truth back there somewhere."

"No, really, I didn't set this up. Tom and Nathan had the contacts, it wasn't me. Those trips I didn't tell you about? It really didn't matter. That was just a little fling I had with an American Airlines pilot who's married and who flew international flights out of Miami, mostly to Europe. He'd get me a free seat, and I'd meet him wherever he had a layover, and we'd screw and have fun. But I got tired of him before Thanksgiving.

"Nathan and Tom were setting up the drug thing then, through contacts Tom made in England. I think, but I'm not sure, that he was forced to do it by someone there who he had cheated on a Bitcoin, or some weird currency thing. I guess you can't cheat on Bitcoin, but this person who Tom cheated, who I never met by the way, was a friend of Aleksei's associate, and Aleksei suggested getting Tom to move drugs as compensation. From what I could piece together, that's what I think happened. And Tom needed Nathan to help do it all."

"Why didn't you tell me this from the beginning?"

"Well then I would have been guilty of withholding evidence wouldn't I? I didn't want to go to jail."

"You're confusing me. You're the one who reported them missing and helped me find the shop where they shipped the drugs out."

"I know, but by then they were both missing, and I knew something was wrong. It wasn't until I came to Europe and found Aleksei that I learned that Tom had planned to cheat the guy again and was trying to divert the drugs and hold them for a sort of ransom. He was an idiot. They figured it out, of course, and killed him.

"I think Nathan is hiding out, I just don't believe he's dead. Mother's instinct, I guess."

"But why is Aleksei looking for you? What does he need you for?"

"Oh, I forgot to mention, some of the drug shipment is still missing, and I told him I'd help him find Nathan, who must have the drugs or know where they are. If he wasn't trying to kill me, I would find him a very attractive man. He's very polite and well-educated and cultured you know. And generous and sexy."

Redd stared in amazement at her and shook his head.

Marta smiled at him. "I just wanted you to know the truth. Maybe you can put in a good word for me when we get back to the States. I didn't really do anything all that wrong." She yawned. "Can I take a little nap now? I'm tired after that dinner. Let me come over and lean on you."

77

Back to Victim

They got to the hotel after midnight and checked in. Redd had booked a deluxe room with two twin beds. They were side by side, but at least had separate bedding. The room was small but adequate. He only expected to be there one night.

Marta said she wanted to take a shower, so Redd left his two bags in the room and went back to the lobby to call Berry and Kathryn. He told Berry briefly what had happened and why he had not been in touch. Berry was not happy with him, but Redd told him he had had to make a decision on the spot, and that he had safely gotten Marta to Paris and would have her back in DC by tomorrow afternoon, as soon as he could book a flight. Berry said he would book the flight for the two of them and text him the info. He would make it a late morning departure and arrange to meet them at Dulles.

Redd then called Kathryn and gave her a brief update. "So, she was not guilty of anything and looking for her missing husband and son, then she's guilty and part of the entire scheme, and now she's back to victim and being hunted by a Russian? You know how ridiculous this sounds, don't you?"

"Yes, and I have no idea which part of any of it is true. I will just be glad to get her back to Berry and out of my hands and out of our lives."

"Where is she now?"

"I booked a room with two beds and left her to take a shower. I'll sleep with my clothes on and one eye open, if I sleep at all. You do trust me, don't you?"

"Oh, I trust you, but I certainly don't trust her. Be careful."

"I will. I love you. I'm anxious to be back."

"I love you, too. See you tomorrow if all goes well."

Redd was surprised how calm Kathryn was about him being with Marta, but she was right to believe in his fidelity to her.

When Redd got back to the room, Marta had finished showering and was in the bed furthest from the door, turned on her side and asleep. Her clothes were draped over an easy chair next to her bed, so Redd assumed she must be sleeping in her underwear or nothing at all. There was a bra draped over the back of the chair.

True to his word, he kept his pants and shirt on, but pulled off his belt and emptied his pockets and laid down on the other bed. He set his phone up to charge and left only the bathroom light on with the door slightly ajar. He settled onto the bed and relaxed, and five minutes later was deeply asleep.

78

With Love

Redd jerked awake. He had been dreaming, struggling to pull himself up the edge of a cliff, and just as he reached a little higher each time, the cliff itself seemed to grow, much further out of his reach. He had been so deeply asleep, it took him a moment to realize where he was. It was too quiet. He had rolled on his side away from the other bed in his sleep, and he turned now and saw that the bed was empty and the clothes from the chair were gone. Marta had slipped out while he slept.

He sat up and turned on the light. His bags were where he had left them, but the zipper on the backpack was undone, and the pistol he had taken from her was gone. If he had been thinking more clearly, he would have put it under his pillow or under the mattress. But he really hadn't considered she might run after she came to him in Prague.

He had no idea how long she had been gone. He picked up the phone on the table by the bed and then noticed a folded piece of paper. He picked it up and read it:

My dear protector Redd, you saved me from danger twice, but you can't save me from myself. I'm sorry to have to leave you like this. I hope it doesn't get you into too much trouble. You are a good man. I wonder what would have happened if I had met you a long time ago. Don't bother to look for me, I'll be a world away. Kathryn is lucky, but so are you. With love, as I understand it. M.

Redd reread the note and smiled to himself. He put it back on the table, pulled off his shirt and pants and got back into bed and fell asleep.

Epilogue

A few weeks later, when the weather had warmed sufficiently that Douglas could leave his house overnight and not have things freeze up when his woodstove burned out, he came to visit Kathryn and Redd for a couple of nights and to look into arrangements for the trip he wanted to take to Belgium to Oudenaarde and to some museums in Paris as well.

While he was visiting, Redd had him look again at the accounts that he had found for Tom McFerren when the investigations first began. Douglas found that the principal had been moved out of the account in the Bahamas to one in Panama, but it had enough security that he couldn't access it. The account had had close to $4 million in it when he had seen it earlier. If you added in the $1.4 million that Marta had had from the sale of the house by Lexington, she should have enough money to hold even her for a good while, assuming she figured out a way to invest it wisely.

Berry had chewed Redd out for letting Marta get away, but Redd had a feeling that Berry was actually relieved to not have to deal with the case any longer. He had Interpol look for her name on flight manifests out of both Paris airports for a few days, but nothing turned up. She had said she would be a continent away, perhaps a stable, friendly country in South or Central America or off to southeast Asia, a country like Thailand which seemed to attract the wanderers.